Moonlit Stalker

Pearl Lake, the Moonlit Trilogy

Book Two

Tina Marie

This is a work of fiction. Names, characters, businesses, places, events, and incidents are either the products of the author's imagination or used in a fictitious manner. Any other resemblance to actual persons, living or dead, or actual events is entirely coincidental.

Moonlit Stalker, Pearl Lake, The Moonlit Trilogy Book 2
Copyright © 2019 Tina Marie
Front Cover Image provided by Bob West
Back Cover Image used under license from Shutterstock

All rights reserved. No part of this book shall be uploaded, reproduced, transmitted or distributed in digital, or paper reproduction without the written consent of the author. If you're wishing to use any part of this book for reviews or articles, please use it in quotations. Thank you for understanding the author's rights.
ISBN: 9798606913107

Dedication

To all my readers who loved One Moonlit Night, the beginning of Abbi and Ben's story. Thank you, thank you, thank you! Words cannot describe how much your support is appreciated. And two special thank yous. To Diane Lieder. As a dedicated reader of the trilogy, your enthusiasm makes my day. And to Bob West, thank you for your photo and making me realize I'm not being picky, I'm being "artistically selective".

Chapter 1

Abbi sat straight up in bed; something had awakened her. Feeling a cool breeze on her chest, she glanced down, and noticed her lack of clothing. She jerked the blankets up to her shoulders. *Good Lord, I've never slept naked in my life...*

For a second she was confused until she felt the bed moving. Then it hit her like a ton of bricks. Memories of Ben and her came flooding back. She had been so… for lack of a better word… wanton. She hadn't known she could even be that way, but she had. And it had felt awesome. She giggled as she nestled into the blankets. She turned her head, watching him while he slept. *He's a gorgeous human being. Kind, sweet, attentive and sexy as hell. And he wants me...* She didn't know if she would ever truly believe that.

Sighing softly, she leaned over and kissed him on the cheek, just as the dogs started freaking out. Not their usual way of communicating, but full-blown *'someone is about to break into the house'* freaking out. She turned to her bedside table and opened the drawer, removing the laptop within.

Turning it on, she sat, waiting for it to boot up.

"Hey love," Ben murmured, rubbing her back.

She turned, looking over her shoulder at him. "Hey handsome," she smiled. "Did you sleep well?"

He moved closer to her, smiling. "As a matter of fact, I did," he murmured, softly brushing his lips along her ribcage.

The laptop came alive with a beep, announcing it was ready. Abbi typed in a password. The screen filled with a live feed from the cameras, inside and out of the house.

"Wow! That's impressive," Ben said, leaning on his arm behind her, looking at the screen.

"Ah... yeah," she concentrated on all the different views. "The dogs are carrying on a bit unusual," she explained, frowning.

Ben sat up; eyes fixed on the screen. Frowning, he pointed to the view of her driveway where a car was parked. "Who is that?" he asked, tapping it.

"Huh... I don't know," she said. She turned her head to get a better view.

He looked closer. His brows pulled together in concentration. "Someone is walking around the car."

Abbi clicked on the screen to enlarge it. She didn't recognize the car. She zoomed in to get a better look of the person... persons; she corrected herself. There were now two of them. Just then, another car pulled into her driveway.

Both leaned forwards, staring at the screen. The people from the second car got out and headed towards the first couple. A moment of horrified realization hit them both at the same time. She tossed the laptop on the bed. Turning towards each other, Ben grabbed Abbi by her shoulders as she grabbed his arms.

"*Bloody HELL!* My parents are *here!*"

"Oh, my *GOD!* My *kids* are here!!!"

They jumped up scrambling for their clothes.

Abbi glanced at him as she pulled on her sweats. "You *cannot* put your pajama pants back on!!!" she hissed.

With one leg in, Ben paused a moment in thought. "Yeah, you're right!!" he said, running for his bag in the other room.

Abbi shoved her arms into her tank top, tugging it over her head. Pulling her sweater on, she noticed her pants were on backwards.

"Aargh," she huffed. Whipping them down, she spun them the right way.

She had no idea where Ben had gone off to. *Hiding if he was smart.* She took a quick glance in the mirror only to see her tousled mop of hair. The memory of Ben's hands in it made her blush terribly. Grabbing a ball cap, she gathered it into a ponytail, stuffing it through the hole in the back. Darting her gaze to the monitor, she saw Ava walking up the sidewalk to the porch.

"Ben!!! Where are you?" she called walking into the hall.

"Right here, Luv." He appeared behind her, zipping up his jeans. He reached out to catch her hand. "Hey," he said pulling her around to face him. "Before we need to deal with this, know that every second that they are here, I'm thinking of you and what we shared." He cupped her neck, his thumb trailed along her jawline as he closed the gap between them, brushing his lips softly against hers.

She kissed him back, desperate to remember the taste of him. The feel of his mouth against her own. It would be hard not to touch him for a week.

The ringing of her doorbell broke them apart. The dogs beat a trail once again to the door, in a frenzy of barks.

He gave her one last longing look before she turned away. She took his hand, leading him into the kitchen.

"Ready?" she asked. Taking a deep breath, she walked to the door.

"Yeah," he gave a quick nod. Smiling he added, "As I'll ever be."

Abbi gripped the handle and opened the door wide. The dogs flew out, clamoring for attention from anyone who would give it.

"Ava, honey." Abbi held out her arms.

"Mom!! It's good to see you. I've missed you," she said,

rubbing her back. "And who is this?"

"The name's Ben," he smiled, offering his hand.

"How nice!" Ava smiled, shaking his hand. "I think I just met your parents. The rest are just talking to them now." She glanced out the door, motioning to the gathered group.

"Yeah, that would be them," he nodded. "Excuse me. Nice to meet you," he said to Ava.

Ben turned to Abbi, his hand going to the small of her back. Softly he said, "I'll be right back, Luv. I'll just greet my parents."

Abbi stepped out onto the porch, watching him approach the group. She watched as his mom turned around. A look of pure heaven crossing her lovely features. She took his face in her hands, kissing him on the cheek. She then glanced at his arm in the brace, covering her mouth when she saw it. She wrapped her arms around him and cried happy tears at the sight of her son. Ben's dad continued to talk to Luke, Lane, and a beautiful girl…. Cassie was it? She couldn't remember.

Her sister, Kim, had broken off from the group walking towards the house, stopping here and there to admire the plants in Abbi's gardens. Ava stepped up beside her mom, putting an arm around her waist. Abbi did the same, pulling her close to her side.

"So… Mom…"

"Yes, sweetie?"

Ava glanced towards her giving her a sidelong stare. Abbi raised her brows in question. "About that, Ben. He's ah…

fine-looking, isn't he?" she grinned.

"I have noticed, yes." Abbi smiled as she watched Ben's dad give him a bear hug. His mother dabbing her eyes as she talked to Cassie.

"His parents are nice too, really informative," Ava said, nodding her head.

"Hmm. Nice. I haven't met them yet."

Abbi furrowed her brows. *What is Ava getting at...* She tried to remember what Ben said to his father on the phone the other day... Wait, that was just yesterday?

Oh my God! He told his dad about us...

"Yeah. They said they just had to come from England to meet the woman who captured their son's heart. Hmm... imagine that." Ava stroked her chin looking at the sky in thought.

Abbi swallowed hard. A golf ball-sized lump in her throat refused to go down. "Really?" she squeaked.

"Mhm... They went to his house after getting directions from Mack. He told them if Ben wasn't at home, he might be here." She moved her arm from Abbi's waist to rest it on her shoulders.

"Nice people they are. I think their English accents are just the cutest thing." Ava grinned. "Especially when they said how nice it was that Ben found a woman who lived right beside him. His girlfriend, if I'm not mistaken. Any new houses being built since the last time we were all together, Mom?" she queried, chuckling and looking around.

"You are a horrible daughter." Abbi laughed, hugging her.

Ava grinned. "A-ha! I'm sorry! I just couldn't help myself. Is he the real deal though, Mom? Or is he after your money?"

Noting Abbi's stern look, Ava backed away, holding out her hands in defense. "Correct me if I'm wrong. I just worry about you... up here all by yourself."

Abbi took her daughter's face in her hands, her eyes softening. "Yes honey, he's the real deal. At least it feels like he is." She kissed the tip of Ava's nose. "And he has his own money too, so please don't worry about that."

If Ava didn't know that he was an actor, it wasn't Abbi's place to tell her. She watched Ben shake hands with Luke then Lane, as his father introduced them. All smiling and happy... for now.

"You're not like... having sex, are you?" Ava asked, searching her mother's face. "Oh... My... God! You *are*!!!" she said, her voice rising with every word. "You lucky bitch!" she laughed.

"Shh!! Keep your voice down. I don't want the entire world to know for goodness sake!" Pointing her finger at her daughter she chided, "And *don't* you *dare* breathe a word about this to anyone. We are keeping our relationship quiet for now."

"Your secret is safe with me." Ava grinned. "But everyone here already knows. Ben's parents spilled the beans, remember?"

"Great... just great," Abbi said dryly. "I wanted to tell Lane. Luke won't care, but you and Lane..." Abbi trailed off shaking her head. Scrunching her forehead, she looked at Ava.

"Why are you guys here, anyway? Lane said Thursday, today is Tuesday."

Abbi could feel the tension seeping in her shoulders. "And Aunt Kim? Lane never mentioned bringing her along." Abbi wondered where everyone would sleep.

Ava gripped her mom's shoulders, massaging the tightness that she knew was there. "We all got off a few days early and wanted to surprise you. Aunt Kim just wanted to tag along," she explained, working on a stubborn knot.

"I'm sorry, honey." Abbi was, she had no cause to snap at Ava like that. "I've just been under a tremendous amount of stress lately," she said, watching Cassie who now joined Kim over by the plants. Abbi followed Cassie's line of sight.

How sweet. She's watching... Nope, that's not who she's looking at.

Ava immediately felt the tension she had just been working to relieve, suddenly return. Something was bothering her mother; she could feel it under her hands. Looking over her mother's shoulder,

she saw exactly what the cause of it was.
Cassie... watching Ben with hunger in her eyes. Ava rested her chin on her mother's shoulder. "Ah, yeah, Mom... you might want to nip that in the bud," she mumbled.

Chapter 2

Ben heard his mom say that his dad, and she had traveled straight from England the minute they had hung up the phone with him yesterday. He didn't doubt it.

"Hey, Mum."

He waited for the onslaught from his mother at the sound of his voice. She stopped in mid-sentence. Turning around, she let out a delighted squeal. Taking hold of his face, she kissed him on the cheek. Nancy backed up, her eyes falling on his arm.

"Oh, my goodness, Benjamin! What happened to you? Did you get attacked by a bear?" she asked. She covered her mouth as the horrible image crossed through her mind.

"No mum," Ben chuckled. "I ah, took a tumble is all. It's good to see you." He meant it; he just wished they had waited a tad longer, or at least given a heads up. His mom hugged him as happy tears spilled from her eyes.

"I've missed you so," she said, rocking him side to side.

Ben glanced over at his dad. "Dad, so good to see you." His mother still hung on tight.

"Nancy, let him go for God's sake."

She took a step back, dropping her arms. She wiped her tears.

"You will drive him up a wall and he'll have us on the first flight back to England." His dad laughed. Stepping forward, he gave his son a hug. "Ben, it's good to see you," Greg said.

Lowering his voice so only Ben could hear he added, "Sorry about all this, she just wouldn't wait and threatened to come by herself."

Ben's eyes lit with amusement; he could picture it. He gave a quick nod and smiled. "It's okay, Dad. I figured as much."

Stepping back, Greg turned to the group gathered.

"Have You met Abbi's sons? Luke and Lane, and is it Luke's girlfriend, Cassie?" he said looking at them for affirmation.

Ben took Luke's hand in a firm grip. It was hard to tell apart the two men standing before him; they were a mirror image of each other. "Hey, how's it going?" he asked.

"Good, man, nice to meet you and I'm Luke."

Ben turned to the other man. "Lane, I take it?" he asked with a grin, shaking his hand.

"Indeed, it is. How's the good old Canadian north treating you?" Lane asked him.

"Good. No complaints so far."

"Nice!" Luke nodded. "Oh, this here is Cassie," he said draping an arm around her shoulders.

Ben squinted as if the sun was streaming in his eyes. It wasn't. He just immediately recognized the look that Cassie was tossing his way. "Pleased to meet you." Ben nodded, not bothering to extend his hand. She murmured a greeting and walked away.

"So, Ben, what is it you do for a living?" Lane asked.

"Ah..." Ben was just about to tell him when Luke interjected.

"Duuude. You *just* met the guy. *REALLY*? You gotta ask that now?" Luke changed the subject. "Let's go say hi to mom, I'm sure she'd just love the break from Ava's interrogation."

Lane looked at Ben apologetically and said, "Sorry, he's right. Mr. and Mrs. Quinn, I'm sure you would like to meet her as well?"

"Oh, of course! It would be a delight," Nancy said striding along with them, tugging Greg's hand behind her. Ben stood there for a second, watching the four of them make their way to the house.

He glanced towards Cassie and a lady he had yet to meet. Cassie was staring at him intently with a come-hither look. He ignored her as he followed the rest to the house.

Abbi's eyes flashed with anger when she saw Cassie giving Ben a smoldering look. Abbi had to deal with a full house for a week, but she also had to deal with Cassie undressing Ben with her eyes. She honestly didn't know if she could handle it without hitting her.
"Mom, you're ravishing as usual," Luke said hugging her.
"And you're still a sweet talker I see," she laughed, wrapping her arms around him.
Lane came up behind Luke reaching out. He, too, gave her a hug and a kiss on the cheek. "Hey mom, how's it going?" he asked, a look of concern on his face as he took hold of her hand.
"Good Honey, it's going well," she said, giving his hand a reassuring squeeze.
Abbi heard Ben's mom whisper to his dad. "Oh my, she is a darling."
Ben stepped forward, taking Abbi's hand in his, he searched her face. He wanted to drop a quick kiss on her lips, but not in front of both their families. Instead, he gave her a slight questioning nod. She returned it with one of her own. He took a deep breath.
"Mum, Dad. I'd like you to meet Abbi Peterson. Abbi my parents, Nancy and Greg Quinn." He inclined his head towards them.
"Nice to meet you both," Abbi said, holding out her hand.
Neither of them took it; both just stood there staring at her. She quickly risked a glance at Ben's face, he seemed to be holding his breath. Abbi saw her kids were too. *Awesome! They hate me...*

She was ready to go jump in the lake when his mother let out a squeal, throwing out her arms for a hug. "Oh, my goodness you sweet, sweet girl, you!!" She grabbed Abbi into the folds of her arms, jumping in place.

Abbi was shocked. *Girl?? Just how old did people look in England? ...*

"Nancy. For God's sake! You will give the girl a headache, let her go!" Greg said laughing. "Come here girl, and let me look at you," Greg said, taking her by the shoulders.

Again, with the girl? His parents are lovely, but are they blind or something?

"Please, excuse Nancy. I fear the jet lag is getting to her a bit. That and we never thought Ben would ever find another girl. Not after what that slag did to him while he was off...." Nancy jabbed him in the ribs.

Luke, Ava, and Lane's brows all shot up at the mention of the word slag. None of them had a clue what it was, but it couldn't be a good thing.

"Dad..." Ben uttered the one word, giving him a 'seriously, shut the hell up' look. Which was enough for Greg to understand it was a warning not to continue. "Abbi already knows what happened, and I would prefer it wasn't talked about anymore," he said looking at them both, smiling to soften his words.

Greg nodded with understanding.

"So, who wants a drink?" Ava asked, clapping her hands.

"Ben? Mr. and Mrs. Quinn? You ready for a drink?" she asked, nodding her head. Not waiting for a response, she turned on her heel and walked into the house.

"Please, call us Nancy and Greg, dear. And that sounds divine," Nancy replied, eagerly tugging Greg's hand as she followed Lane and Ava into the house.

"Luke, can you grab Aunt Kim," Ava yelled. She scrunched up her nose. "And... what's her name again?"

"Cassie, for the tenth time, Ava," Luke said, shaking his head.

"Oh yeah, that's right. Grab her too," she called.

"Well... hellooo, stranger," Abbi heard Kim saying to Ben.

She turned to see her sister climbing the steps with Luke and Cassie hot on her heels.

"Well, hello to you too, stranger," Ben grinned.

"Ben, this is my sister, Kim," Abbi said, monitoring Cassie.

She needn't feel jealous. Well, hell, yeah, she should! Here was this young thing, openly showing interest in Ben. She looked like she was about to pounce on him any minute. The kicker... Luke was standing next to her.

Kim opened her arms in a way of greeting him. "Get over here, big boy!" she chuckled.

Ben let out a bark of laughter. "Ah..." he looked to Abbi for help. *What should I do?* ... His eyes pleaded with her to give him the knowledge.

"Oh, I get it. You're a one-woman man, aren't you, stud," she said giving him a wink. "Good. Nothing but the best for my baby sister." Kim turned her head around. She locked eyes with Cassie. "You two take a lesson from this man. Now, let's get our drink on." Kim stepped aside to let them her and Lane pass. Muttering out the side of her mouth, Kim pointed to Cassie's back.

"Keep an eye on that one." She looked pointedly at Ben and Abbi as she sauntered after the two.

Ben reached in and closed the door, shutting them off from the others inside. He took Abbi's hand and led her a few feet away from it. "Do you think if we left and went to my house, they would notice us gone?" he laughed, taking her into his arms.

Abbi smiled up at him. "Hmm, we can try. That didn't go so

bad, I think."

She was happy that they didn't have to hide their feelings now. That would have been pure torture if they had to.

Ben stood still in thought, he nodded, pursing his lips. "Yeah, not too bad. My parents like you a lot."

"The feeling is mutual," she smiled. "The kids hit it off with you okay?"

"Seemed to." He nodded. "I've missed you," he murmured against her lips. Pressing the small of her back, he drew her towards him and showed her exactly how true that was. Her eyes flashed with desire, causing him to groan with frustration.

Wrapped up in one another, neither of them heard the door open. Ava poked her head out. "Hey, you two. Aren't you guys coming... Whoa! Good, God! Get a room, will you?" she said slamming the door.

Her reaction mortified Abbi. "We shouldn't have done that," she pulled herself out of Ben's arms.

Ben didn't reach for her this time. "Abbi, she's an adult. I'm sure she doesn't expect her mother to be single for the rest of her life, does she?" he reasoned.

"No. I don't think she does." Motioning with her hand, she said, "She knows about us... You know... *US!*"

He squinted his eyes in thought. "You mean she knows that we've made love, is that what you mean?"

Just above a whisper, she replied, "Yeah." Abbi laid a hand on his chest. "I didn't tell her. She just guessed it."

He took her hand in his, kissing it. "Good. Luv, I will shout it to the world if you want me to," he said, grinning.

"*Noo!*" she punched him playfully on his good arm. "You wouldn't dare."

"Try me." He winked at her.

Laughing, she ran to the door. Her hand stilled on the doorknob. "Ready?" She asked.

"As I'll ever be," he answered with a heavy sigh.

Chapter 3

They finished supper and were sitting down by the lake around a bonfire. Ben was on one side of Abbi, Ava on the other. She glanced across the fire at his parents and marveled at how sweet they were to each other. They were sitting hand in hand, talking in hushed tones. She watched as Nancy bent to kiss Greg. He looked swiftly around to see if anyone noticed. Abbi smiled. *Ben doesn't get his forwardness from his dad...*

Luke interrupted her thoughts. "Mom how is the book coming along?" he asked, poking the fire with a stick.

"Oh, good!" she nodded. "I hit a wall for a bit there, just needed some inspiration was all." She looked at Ben. He was her inspiration.

Nancy leaned forward, smiling. "You're a writer? How exciting! Do you write romance novels by any chance? I do so love a good romance."

Abbi winced, glancing at Ben for help. He was sitting there with his elbow resting on the back of her chair, his head in his hand. "Um... not exactly," she said, "I write..."

"She writes about murder mum," Ben supplied. Looking at Abbi, he shot her a wink and a soft smile.

Abbi looked at him, her eyes growing large. *He could have been a tad more tactful.*

"Ha! Right up my alley," Greg interjected.

Nancy looked as if she just ate a frog or sucked on a lemon. Abbi wasn't entirely sure which.

"What's the name of your book, dear?" Greg asked, genuinely interested.

Abbi smiled. "The Jasper Killings."

"The Jasper Killings?" Greg looked around in thought. "Where have I heard that name before? I haven't read it, but the title is very familiar," he said, tapping his chin with a finger.

Ben had a moment of panic. He didn't care if the others knew about him being an actor. But he didn't want Cassie to know. She had her phone in her hand most of the night, which was perfectly fine by him. At least when she was looking at it, she wasn't trying to catch his attention. Every time he glanced over to talk to Luke, she was staring at him. He'd bet money on it... the second she found out he was in movies; it would hit the social media sites. Something that he didn't want.

"Say, Dad," Ben said standing up. He jerked a thumb towards the garden shed, his brows raised. "Can you come and have a look at Abbi's power washer with me for a minute? We can't seem to get it running."

"Sure thing! Would love to tinker with it." Greg jumped up, coming to stand beside Ben.

Abbi glanced around at him. *What the hell is he talking about?*

Ben put his hand on her shoulder, giving her a gentle squeeze. "Love, can you get the keys?" he asked, nodding at her.

"Aww, how sweet? He called you love, Mom," Ava hiccupped, looking down into her empty glass.

Abbi got up, heading to the house. Her kids' happy banter trailing her as she did.

"Have a little one too many, there Ava?" Lane burst out laughing, with Luke joining in.

Abbi was halfway to the house when Ben caught up to her, steering her away to the bushes where no one could see them.

"What are you doing?" she asked, giggling.

"This." He planted his lips on hers, hungrily.

"Where is your dad?" she asked breathlessly, tearing her mouth from his.

He jerked his head back, biting his lip as his eyes twinkled at her. "Standing at the shed waiting for us."

"You're terrible," she said laughing, shaking her head.

"Come on. I'll walk with you." He linked his fingers with hers.

Once in the house, he ran to the bathroom while she rummaged in the junk drawer in the kitchen for the keys.

"Aha!" she held the keys up triumphantly. She saw a flash of pain cross his face as he walked back into the kitchen.

"How's your shoulder doing?"

"The pain is a mild ache now. Earlier, I could have ripped someone's head off. But the beer seems to have dulled it now," he said, leaning against the counter.

"Remind me and I'll call Doc Spence tomorrow. He said he'd try to get some other pain meds for you brought in from Springbank."

She gathered the makings for s'mores. Just in case, she grabbed a bag of chips and a box of cookies as well.

At the mention of the doctor, Ben's thoughts turned to everything that had happened in the past few days. Sure, both of their families were here, so the likelihood of something else happening was slim. But he still hadn't called the police about it. *Mark! He'd know who to contact.* If Ben remembered correctly, his brother was a cop. He itched to call him this minute.

"You ready to go open the shed now for your dad? He must be sick of waiting." Abbi looked at him, noticing he was deep in thought.

She put the items on the counter. "Hey. What's wrong?" she asked.

She went behind him. Placing her hands on his neck, rubbing away his tension.

"Nothing." He turned around to look at her, dropping a quick kiss on the tip of her nose.

She knew something was up, but clearly, he didn't want to talk about it. Nor did she press him. "Are you coming?" Her brows rose with the question.

"Yeah. Uh… I'll be right there in a bit; you go on ahead." He nodded towards the lake. Ben saw the flash of concern on her beautiful face. He wanted to tell her what he was up to but doing so would only make her worry. Something he didn't want her to do. She gave a quick nod and walked into the living room and out the door without a word.

He let out a heavy sigh watching her as she approached his dad. She must have said something funny because his dad was roaring with laughter. Ben grabbed his cell from his back pocket. Looking at his caller's list, he connected to Mark's number.

"Mark buddy! It's Ben. I got a favor to ask you." He laughed. "No, Abbi isn't free to date you. No this is serious; you got a minute…?"

"Hi, Greg! Here are the keys," she said, handing them to his dad. "Um, I'm not sure which one it is. I just keep trying until I get the right one. Funny how it's always the last one," she shrugged.

Greg looked at the ring she handed him. There had to be at least thirty keys on it. He threw his head back, barking like a seal. Abbi joined in; she couldn't help herself; his laughter was so contagious.

Grinning, she said, "I'll be right back, just going to give these to them."

She set off towards the fire.

"Here Lane," she handed him the bag of marshmallows and sat the rest on a chair.

"Right on." He got up collecting branches off a nearby tree.

"Nancy, do you need anything?" Abbi asked her.

"No thank you, dear. I'm just sitting here all toasty and warm," she said, dreamily staring at the flames.

The loons were out on the lake now, calling to each other. Nancy turned in her chair, looking at the lake. "What in the world is that glorious sound?" she asked.

"That's just the loons," Lane answered, offering a fist full of sticks to everyone. Abbi zoned out as he explained exactly what loons were to Nancy. She glanced around. Ava was just about passed out in her chair. Luke was on his phone. Kim and Cassie were nowhere to be seen. *Maybe they went for a walk...* She turned around and headed back to Greg.

As she approached, she heard him talking to someone, expecting it to be Ben. Abbi was mildly shocked when Kim was bent over, looking at the power washer. "Hey, you two, where is Cassie?"

"Ah, I saw her go up to the house a few minutes ago," Kim said, untangling the power cord.

Abbi glanced at the house... Ben was in there... alone. She took off at a fast walk, jogging the rest of the way to the house. She suddenly stopped just at the top of the steps. *Do I want to see what is going on in there?* ... She trusted Ben, thinking back to the time when they went shopping and how he acted around those girls.

That's just it Abbi… acted, he is an actor… There was no stopping her from going into her own home. She'd sneak quietly into the living room; sticking close to the wall so they wouldn't see her.

If nothing was going on, she could easily slip right back out, none the wiser.

Ben was explaining to Mark exactly everything that had happened since he had last seen him.

"Right. So, all he'd need is the last name to go with the first and he could trace him?" He could hear someone walking around the house, thinking it was Abbi coming in from her bedroom entrance. He needed to change the subject fast, he didn't want her knowing why he was talking to Mark.

"So yeah." he cleared his throat. "When are you coming back this way?"

The footsteps were coming into the kitchen now.

"Really, that's great! Why don't you pop over on the weekend then? Abbi's family is here and so are my parents."

Ben could feel her hand on his back, causing him to smile. It felt wonderful. Wait, no it didn't. Whipping around he saw Cassie standing there, a smile on her painted lips.

"Bloody hell!" he yelled.

"No Mark, not you! Just come over on the weekend. Right? I'll see you then."

He stuck his phone in his back pocket as he glared at Cassie. Anger flashed from his eyes. "Just what the hell do you think you're doing?" he asked.

Abbi could hear Ben on the phone with Mark. She was about to leave when she heard him say goodbye. Then he yelled 'bloody hell'. She had every intention of hightailing it outside, thinking he'd caught her in the act, until she heard him ask what the hell someone thought they were doing. She stopped in her tracks. *It could only be Cassie...*

Abbi had heard enough, she had to get Luke. Damn it, the lake was so far. She was bound to miss something.

Turning on her heel, she snuck towards the porch. Luckily, she didn't have far to go. Luke was coming up the back steps. She motioned for him to stop and placed a finger to her lips. She grabbed his arm and together they snuck in along the wall and waited.

"I saw you looking at me all night," Cassie said advancing towards Ben, like a lion stalking its prey.

Ben backed away. He snickered. "Uh, no you didn't." He moved to put the counter between them. Clearly, the woman was delusional. He needed to get out of there fast.

"Yes, I did. I've been watching you from the moment we arrived. I know you want me," she said seductively, lunging at him. She wrapped her arms around his neck, pulling him close, aiming her mouth at his.

Ben turned his head to avoid contact with her lips. His glance fell on the box of cookies. Snatching the box up he promptly covered his face with it. He could hear Cassie sputtering as her mouth met the box.

Abbi's brows shot up when they heard a rustling sound followed by what sounded like Cassie spitting out a mouthful of dirt.

"I love a man who plays hard to get," she heard Cassie growl.

"Look, Cassie. Believe me when I tell you, I have no inclination *whatsoever* to play hard to get with you." He removed her hands from around his neck and stepped away from her, inching slowly back towards the living room.

"First off. You must be blind to not notice I'm with Abbi, something I take seriously." He stepped back another inch.

He had to deal with women like this before and knew at any second it could get ugly.

"Blinded by your sexiness," she crooned, tossing her hair.

Ben ignored her comment. "Second, you're not my type and thirdly you're with Luke."

He had thought he had finally gotten through to her until she said, "So you mean I still have a chance?" A lecherous grin spread on her thin lips.

Abbi was just about to jump out and slug the bitch, but Luke caught hold of her waist. Shaking his head, he motioned for her to stay. Her eyes flashing fire, she gave him a pointed look as she headed back towards the porch.

Cassie's lips reminded Ben of earthworms, skinny earthworms. He physically gagged at that thought. "Are you *daft,* woman?"

Luke couldn't have chosen a better word himself. He stepped out from behind the wall. "Hey, Ben. Need some help?" Luke tossed Cassie a disgusted look.

Ben turned, relief flooding his face. He nodded and said, "Thanks, man," as he took off through the living room and outside in search of Abbi.

Chapter 4

He didn't need to go far. She was leaning up against the porch railing, her hands folded across her chest. From the looks of her stance, he knew she had heard what happened in there.

"Hey love," he softly said. Reaching out, he smoothed her hair away from her face.

"Hey." She glanced at him. "Walk with me?" she asked, catching his hand.

He looked into her eyes. "Always," he murmured, kissing her softly on the lips.

Neither of them said a word as they headed to the shed. His dad and Kim were still in there working on the power washer. Ben looked down at it. "Hey, dad... that's not broken."

Greg frowned. "Well. It is now. We will have another go at it tomorrow when it's daylight."

Ben glanced between his dad and Kim. "I'm sorry about that. I just needed an excuse to get you away from there."

"Why ever would you say that it was broke?" Kim asked, the wrench she was holding clanged to the cement floor. "Couldn't you have just said, 'Hey dad come look at Abbi's piece of shit power washer?'... No offense," she said, looking at Abbi.

Abbi laughed at her sister. "None taken." Oh, how she loved that woman's forwardness.

"I didn't want my dad to let it slip." Ben shoved a hand through his hair.

Kim scrunched up her face, trying to figure out what the hell Ben was going on about. "Does he always talk in circles?" she asked.

Looking up in thought, Abbi responded first. "hmm... Nope." She shook her head, smiling.

Greg nodded, chuckling. "Yeah, most of the time."

Ben rubbed the tension from the back of his neck. "I didn't want my dad letting it slip where he heard about Abbi's book," he told Kim.

Greg looked as confused as Kim did Abbi thought with amusement shining in her eyes.

"The Jasper Killings rings a bell to you because it's the movie I'm filming, Dad," he explained, draping his arm around Abbi's shoulders.

"What! You... You're an actor?" Kim stammered, with shock on her face.

Greg piped up. "Yes, he is. And a damn fine one too!" he said, beaming proudly.

"Wait... So that means. You're in Abbi's book?"

"Technically speaking, no," Ben interrupted. It didn't matter; Kim was on a roll.

"Holy crap! You bagged a hottie here, didn't you Abbi?" Kim hooted with laughter, causing Abbi to blush three shades of red.

"Wait till I tell the kids!" she said, bounding towards the lake.

"No, please don't do that. I don't want Cassie finding out." Ben told them the reason for the secrecy. "And that's why I asked you to look at this, Dad." He motioned to the power washer.

"Got you loud and clear." Kim nodded. Out of the corner of her mouth, she said, "She is a bit of a hussy, if you ask me."

Abbi tugged on her shirt. "Kim, please don't say anything to her. I don't want to upset Luke." *Any more than he already is...*

Kim looked at her. "Abbi, I won't. It's not my place to."

She might think differently if she knew what just happened in the house... Ben thought.

Greg offered his arm to Kim. "Shall we return to the fire and back to my lovely wife?" he asked.

"Why certainly, dear chap," Kim mimicked his accent. Taking him by the arm, she turned and said over her shoulder, "I need to find me a British man... Onward, Gregory," she pointed. Her cackle of laughter echoing across the lake.

"Your sister is quite something isn't she?" Ben looked down, smiling at Abbi as they walked to join everyone down by the fire.

"She certainly is a hoot at times, I'll give her that," she nodded in agreement.

Taking their seats, Lane reached out and handed the marshmallows to Ben along with a stick. He held up one for Abbi. "Mom?" he offered. Shaking her head, she declined.

Ava's loud snoring had her looking down. The poor girl was lying on the ground sound asleep. Which led her to wonder where everyone else would sleep. She wasn't expecting Cassie and Kim coming along too. She only had her bedroom and the spare. There were two couches as well, but they weren't very comfortable to sleep on.

Ben leaned over and whispered in her ear. "Hey, love. I think I'll take my parents back to my house." He inclined his head towards his mom. "She's beat, she'll never admit it though."

"Why don't they just stay here. They can sleep in my room," Abbi offered.

He raised his brows in surprise. "You would really give up your bed for them?" he asked her softly.

"Of course, I would!" Standing up, she bent down to brush her lips against his temple. "Just let me go change the bedding first," she murmured.

A shiver went up along his spine at the mention of the bedding. "I'll be there in a minute. I'll just tell my parents and then come and help you."

She looked into his eyes. "You don't have to. It will take no time at all," she said.

"No, I want to. Besides, we need to figure out where everyone else will be sleeping."

"Okay. I'll see you soon then." She smiled, turning away.

Ben watched her disappear into the darkness. He heard a sharp whistle… her call for the dogs to follow, all three bounding after her. Pulling himself out of his chair, he walked over to his parents and crouched down. His mother was dozing off at this point, gently he shook her arm. "Mom, wake up."

"I'm awake dear, just resting my eyes," she mumbled, snoring softly as she drifted off back to sleep.

He turned his attention to his dad. "Dad, do you think you can wake her enough to get her in the house? Abbi is changing the bedding. You guys can sleep in her room tonight."

"Sure thing." Greg nodded. "It may take a few minutes, but we will be there right shortly."

"Sounds good, I'm going to give Abbi a hand. When you come up, just hang a right on the porch to the French doors. They lead to Abbi's room."

Ben jogged up to the house, sailed up the steps and followed the porch to Abbi's room. He quietly entered through the French doors, soundlessly closing the door behind him. Walking through the entryway, he stopped at the sight of her. She was standing with her back to him, hugging the sheets to her chest. A soft smile played on his lips. *What is she doing?*

She inhaled deeply; her face buried in the sheets. Ben turned his head to the side, watching her. "What are you doing?"

Startled, Abbi whipped the sheets to the floor as if they were a snake. She spun around. A blush on her cheeks. "Must you sneak up on me like that?"

He walked to her, taking her in his arms. "Truly, I'm sorry." He arched a brow in question and chuckled. "But were you just sniffing the sheets?"

"No." She looked guiltily away, her eyes darting around the room.

"Yeah, you were," he teased. "I caught you."

She gave him a quick kiss. "Yep, you did. Now help me make the bed before your parents get in here."

Together they made short work of getting the bedroom ready for his parents. Abbi went into the bathroom, putting out clean towels and was just coming out as they knocked on the doors.

"Oh, my! What a lovely room. I do want to thank you, Abbi, for giving up your bed for us. It's very sweet of you," Nancy said, looking longingly towards it.

"You're welcome. Um, did you bring any luggage?" Abbi asked.

"Right! It's out in the car," Greg remembered. "Ben, can you give me a hand?"

Nodding, Ben followed his dad out in the hall.

"Nancy, the bathroom is just through that door," Abbi pointed. "Please, make yourself at home and have a bath if you like."

Nancy sat on the edge of the bed, patting the spot beside her. "Abbi, do you mind sitting with me for a minute, please?"

Oh, no... A feeling of dread came over Abbi at her request.

She just knew his mother secretly disapproved of Ben and her. "Ah sure. I can do that."

She sat beside Nancy. Taking a calming breath, she tried to steady her nerves. If his mom hated her, now was the time for her to say it.

"Dear, I don't know how to put this." Nancy paused. "So, I'll just say it. I've been watching you tonight with my son.

The way you two look at each other reminds me of how Greg and I were when we first met."

Abbi didn't dare say a word.

"I had my doubts of Ben ever finding a love like ours." Nancy sadly shook her head.

Now Abbi spoke. "Ah, with all due respect Nancy. I'm not sure what we have going on is love. I mean we only met, not even a month ago." Abbi stood up. She could no longer sit still and began to pace. "Honestly, I've had reservations about Ben and me," she stopped looking at his mother. "With You and Greg, I'm sure you had normal lives. Ben's isn't normal. In fact, it's the polar opposite."

She started to pace again. "We've talked about it and yes, he was very reassuring. But I mean, come on! He meets glamourous women every single day." Abbi pointed at her chest. "I'm forty-five, with three kids around his age. And a house full of animals, what the hell does he see in me?" She felt like a fool baring her heart out to his mother. "I'm sorry. I shouldn't have said anything." She sat heavily on the bed.

Nancy put a comforting arm around her shoulders. "Perhaps Dear. But I know my son. He may not be in love with you right now, but he loves you. The girl he was with before. They never showed affection to one another at all... ever.

I've never seen him this happy before, not even when he got the part for your book."

Abbi looked at her in surprise. "Oh, Greg must have told you," she stated.

Nancy smiled sweetly. "Not at all. I just looked on the internet when Ben told me he got the part. Of course, it led me right to you... I would say that it was fate that you two met, wouldn't you agree?"

"I never thought of that before." Abbi wasn't one to believe in fate, but she had to admit it seemed like the stars were certainly lining up for them to meet.

The men returned just then carrying the luggage in.

"Mom, what the hell did you pack in here that weighs a ton?" Ben grunted, setting the suitcases down with a bang.

"The kitchen sink," Greg replied, rubbing his back.

They all laughed except Nancy.

"We'll let you two get some rest." Ben said, watching as Abbi came to him. She said, "Goodnight you two," as she closed the door.

They both leaned against the wall between the bedroom doors in the hallway. Abbi glanced at Ben. "Now where is everyone else going to sleep?" she asked softly.

"Well, Kim dragged Ava into the spare room." He jerked a thumb over his shoulder at the closed door. "And Luke and Lane took the couches."

"Okay. So where is Cassie?" she asked.

"Right! Luke told me he called a cab, sent her to Springbank to catch a bus back home," he told her, folding his arms across his chest.

She covered her mouth in disbelief. "No! He didn't?"

"So, you know what this means, don't you?" he asked, giving her a sly grin.

She raised her brows in question. He led her down the hall, through the kitchen, and out the front door, closing it softly behind him. He put his arm around her shoulders as he directed her down the steps. On the ground, he turned to look at her. The moon shining on her face lit up her eyes, eyes that he fell in love with the very first time she laid them on him. He placed his hand at the back of her neck, cradling her head.

"It means my love; we have my house to ourselves." He kissed her with a hunger that they both were feeling; a need to be closer, to be one. Pulling away, he whispered against her soft lips. "Let's get out of here, now!"

They started to run for his house when Abbi suddenly stopped. "Wait, shouldn't we leave a note?"

Bending down Ben said, "Already taken care of. Get on."

"Huh... what?"

"Get on my back. I'll give you a ride."

"Are you crazy?" she laughed.

"Only for you my love," he said, waiting for her to climb on.

"What about your shoulder?"

"It's just a short distance now," he answered, patiently waiting.

"But..."

"Woman! Would you just get on already?!" He asked, laughing at her.

"Fine!" She climbed on, feeling giddy, like a schoolgirl. He jostled her into position as he walked.

"Oh, my!" Her eyes grew large when she felt his hands cover her bottom. "You are a devil, aren't you" she kissed his neck, running her fingers through his hair.

"This is nothing, just you wait."

She smiled at that as he set her down on the porch long enough to unlock the door. Once inside, he turned to lock the door. Abbi stood in the middle of the kitchen, suddenly feeling sick in the pit of her stomach. *What if this all ends, what if he finds someone else, someone young...*

Ben turned to look at her, concern replaced the desire in his eyes. He slowly approached her; she had the look of a deer caught in the headlights.

He gently brushed her cheek with the back of his hand.

"What's the matter, Abbi?" he asked her softly, searching her face.

"I'm not sure, honestly." She felt anxious or was it just excitement? She wasn't sure; it had been so long since she felt pure joy like this. She was afraid of it all slipping from her fingers forever... never, ever feeling this way again.

"Are you sure?" he asked, rubbing her arms. His eyes softened as he looked at her.

"No. I know what it is. I'm not sure I can talk about it just yet," she answered, looking at the floor.

Lifting her chin, he gazed into her eyes. "Is there anything I can do to help?"

She wanted to yell at him, to tell him to never leave her. But she dared not. She couldn't control him, nor did she want to. *I feel like crying... again, damn it! Why does this man do this to me?* Nodding her head, she cleared her throat. "Just hold me please," she mumbled.

He gazed deeply into her eyes as he took her into his arms, his breath hot on her neck. "Would you believe I've been thinking about this all day?" he pulled her closer.

"I've wanted to feel you..." His hand went to the small of her back, pressing her hips to his, "... to taste you." His tongue flicked to the sensitive spot behind her ear.

She gasped as his teeth grazed her skin. Uncontrollable shivers passed through her body. Leaning back against his arm, she bared her neck to his seeking lips. Ben inhaled deeply. His voice was full of desire as he seduced her with his words. "... To smell our mingled scent that only we can create."

Dear God... If anyone ever tried to take this man from her, she feared she'd end up in a prison cell for the rest of her life.

Taking his face in her hands, she brought his mouth to hers. She was going to hell; she knew it. What she felt for him was shameless… to some even sinful. But damn it, it was about time she felt like this. Some people never did, and if she was going to hell for it than she damn well was going to enjoy the ride there.

Ben clung to her lips. A low groan erupting from deep within his throat as he backed her up against the wall. Taking the hem of his shirt, she tugged it over his head, needing to feel his skin against her. She ran her hands down his chest, reveling over the muscles that played below the surface of his smooth skin.

He leaned his head against the wall, breathing heavily as he felt Abbi's mouth scorch down his body. He sucked in a ragged breath as her lips touched his abs, causing them to tighten in response to her seeking mouth. Her hands reached to his jeans, pulling the button loose. As she tugged on the zipper, she could feel the heat coming off him.

He knew full well that if she followed with her mouth, he'd lose all control. As much as he hated to stop her, he had to. Grabbing her hands, he brought her up to meet his mouth. He guided her to his bedroom, their lips clung with every step they took as he peeled off her sweater.

Abbi stopped him at the foot of the bed, shoving him so he sat down on the edge. She stood before him, slowly undressing. She saw the fire leap into his eyes as he licked his lips, leaning back.

He crooked a finger at her. "Come here," he murmured, his voice thick with desire.

She crawled on him as he guided her head, bringing her mouth to his in a frenzy of passion. His other hand drew circles over her breast, teasing it to a peak, that she thought would surely burst. His mouth replaced his hand, biting and lapping. The fiery ache he caused, filled her to her very core.

She felt like screaming as she held him fast to her chest. She needed to do something, anything to stop the sweet torture his mouth was doing to her.

She straddled his hips, pushing him back onto the bed. She met him there with her mouth, tasting the sheen on his body. Moving her bottom to his thighs, she moved her hands once again to his pants, this time he made no move to stop her. She shimmied her way down his legs, pulling his clothes along as she did. She laid down beside him, her eyes even with his hips, taking in her fill of what was before her.

With a feather touch, she took one finger and ran it down his chest, trailing over his stomach and further down. How she loved that trail of hair that dipped down below his bellybutton. She trailed wispy wet kisses there, her reward from him was a guttural groan of agony. Her lips continued their path, making her way to the base of his… she glanced at it. Penis was such an ugly word for such a beautiful thing that created such an intense pleasure within her; she'd decide on a better name for it later. For now, she tenderly placed her lips on that wonderful tip that he had so skillfully teased her with before. She opened her mouth taking him in, swirling her tongue around the edge.

Clenching his jaw, Ben growled out, "Abbi! For the love of God, you need to stop!"

She glanced up meeting his fevered eyes, his veins standing out on his neck from restraining himself. "Are you sure?" she whispered; her breath hot against his already fevered skin.

"No! Yes! You're driving me bloody insane!"

With one last touch to it with her lips, she drew herself up. Straddling his hips, she gently seated herself over him. He groaned loudly as he felt her warm wetness encase him. Grabbing her hips, he held her to him, impaling her with his shaft.

She arched her back when she felt his hand glide to her breast. He sat up wrapping his arms around her while his mouth replaced his hand once again. She rode him as if the very hounds of hell were at her back. She could feel him shudder under her touch. She was in control this time, bringing them together to the edge of the universe in a blast of shimmering stars. She collapsed on him. Their ragged breathing slowly returned to normal. She rested her chin on his chest, with tears in her eyes, she inhaled deeply.

"I see now what you meant when you said about our mingled scent." She gave him a watery smile.

"Yeah?" He kissed her on the forehead. Laying a hand on her hair, he guided her head to his chest.

Soon after he felt her warm tears on his skin as he rubbed her back. "Go to sleep, my love."

He pulled the blanket over them. Drawing her tightly in his arms. He knew he never wanted to be with anyone else for the rest of his life. His final thoughts before sleep claimed him was how to convince her of that.

Chapter 5

Ben was standing in the middle of Abbi's kitchen. His parents sat at the table, sipping their tea while they played a game with Kim, Abbi, and her kids. He was watching her. She had woven a spell over him, around his heart. He was falling in love with her more and more as each day passed. She was laughing and carrying on with them, sitting there in old sweats, her hair up in a messy bun, makeup-free, oblivious to her own beauty. She glanced at him then, a soft smile on her lips. Yeah, he was falling for her... hard.

The need to protect her was maddening; four days had passed since their families arrived. Three days since he found the name of her stalker, Jacob Randal, on her computer. A quick internet search brought up thousands, too many to glean any information to narrow it down. He had immediately contacted Mark with the name and all the information in the file. Mark said the second he heard anything he'd call him; he was still waiting. Mark said he'd stop by today. The waiting was driving Ben crazy. Soon, Abbi would sense something was up. He just didn't want to face her questioning when that happened.

Ben took his cell out of his pocket. Checking to see if he missed a call. He inwardly groaned. As usual, there was nothing. He checked his email, just in case, and saw that Tony had messaged him two days ago. Opening it, Ben frowned as he started reading: *Hey Ben, hope all is well! As luck would have it, it looks like we will start up in a week. Will need you back here in two weeks, if all is a go. Will be in touch, Tony.*

Great, just what we needed... He felt like telling Tony he couldn't possibly make it in two weeks. But doing so would be in breach of his contract. What if they couldn't catch whoever was responsible for the shit that was happening? Sure, it could be this Jacob guy, but what if it wasn't? How was he supposed to protect Abbi from clear across the world?

"Ha....!" Ava gave high fives to Nancy, Kim, and Greg. She looked to Abbi and her brothers, a triumphant gleam in her eyes. "We won! You guys owe us a meal."

"That's because it was four against three... how is that fair?" Lane laughed at her.

"Doesn't matter, losers feed the winners."

"Whiners, you mean?" Luke ducked, laughing, as Ava sent a smack his way.

"Fine, we get to pick the menu," Luke nodded. "Pizza it is." he whipped out his cell.

Just then, all three dogs perked their ears up. Brutus raced towards the door and let out a woof as the doorbell rang.

Abbi's brows shot up. "Huh. He's getting much better at that. Brutus, back up." She tugged on his collar as she opened the door.

"Abbi, sweets! How're you doing, girl?" Mark grabbed her in his arms as he did a jig across the threshold and into the room.

"Mark! Good! Nice to see you again," she laughed, genuinely happy to see him.

He spun her out of his arms as Ben approached him. "Benny boy! My man! How's it going?" Mark asked, hugging him. He smacked Ben on the back. "I got the goods," he muttered, giving Ben a serious look as he backed up.

Immediate relief washed over Ben as he leaned against the counter, drawing Abbi to him.

She leaned back against his solid length, holding onto his hands around her waist.

Mark turned to the table, he walked to it with a smile on his face. "Hi there, Mrs. and Mr. Q… What are you guys doing on this side of the pond?" He asked, as he took Nancy's hand and placed a quick kiss on the back of it.

"Oh Marcus, what are you going on about?" she giggled.

"You know you're the only woman for me," he smiled saucily, winking at her.

"Mark, how are you doing, son?" Greg stood up, folding Mark in a bear hug.

"Good Greg! Just got back from Cali. Needed some R and R, know what I'm saying?"

"That I do, that I do."

Mark glanced to the next person sitting at the table. "And who are you? Wait! Don't tell me, you must be Abbi's sister?" He held out a hand, bowing slightly.

Taking his proffered hand, Kim let out a cackle. "That I am, you cheeky bastard. I'm Kim," she said, studying his face intently.

Luke leaned across the table, offering his hand. "I'm Luke, Abbi's oldest."

Mark took his hand in a firm grip, he glanced to the right of Luke doing a double take. His brows shot up it in surprise. "Whoa! For a minute there I thought you were sitting beside a mirror," he laughed, taking Lane's hand in a firm grip.

"Lane… pleased to meet you." Lane nodded, a smile tugging his lips.

Kim butted in. "Say, why do you look so familiar? Are you from around here?" she asked Mark.

Mark turned to Ben; his brows raised in question. "I don't know. Why do I look so familiar Ben?"

They had an agreement. Whenever either of them met someone new in the presence of each other, they never gave away who they were unless the other was fine with it. Ben gave him the go-ahead with a nod of his head.

Mark turned back to Kim. "Ah... erm... no. Not really from around here, per se. I'm Canadian that is. I sold Ben my house, and we're co-workers..." He was about to tell her where they co-worked at, when a ravishing young lady stepped in the room.

"Oh my God!!" Ava pointed at Mark "You... you, you're... Mark Donovan!" She started jumping up and down, squealing with excitement.

"Who?" Kim said, wrinkling her forehead in confusion.

"You know! The movie we saw last year together." She spun to look at Kim. "What was it called? You know..." Ava said snapping her fingers. "You said it was boring and fell asleep? The people in front of us were pissed because you were snoring so loud."

Ben snorted out a laugh. He knew exactly the movie she was trying to remember. "Delusion," Ben supplied, grinning.

"That's it!" Ava yelled, pointing to Ben.

"Huh..." Kim said, finally remembering the movie. No wonder, she had fallen asleep.

Mark gave Ava a bland look. "Yes, that was one of my worst movies to date. Anyway, pleased to meet you. And you are?" he hedged for her name.

"Ava... my name is Ava... Abbi's daughter," she smiled sweetly... "Wait, so if you two are co-workers..." Ava looked between Ben and Mark. "What is it you do, Ben?" she asked.

There was no need in hiding his job now, with Cassie out of the picture. "I'm an actor. The two of us are filming your mom's book. Well, on break right now, but will head back in a couple of weeks." Ben sighed heavily, glancing down at Abbi.

She tilted her head up at him. A look of sadness in her eyes. "I got the email today," he told her quietly, tightening his arms around her.

She knew it was only a matter of time before he had to leave. She hated the thought of him going; she honestly didn't know what she'd do without him here.

"You have got to be shitting me." Ava let out a laugh. "How..." she was at a loss for words.

"We shit you not! Scout's honor." Mark held up his hand, giving the universal hand signal.

"Wait... How can you know about me, but not Ben?" Mark wondered out loud. "He's a hell of a lot more famous than me."

Ava just shrugged her shoulders, not knowing the answer to his question.

The doorbell rang, announcing the pizza delivery. Luke got up to answer the door, pulling his wallet from his pocket, as he flung the door open.

"Mark, will you stay for dinner?" Ava asked, clearly starstruck. "I mean if you have no other plans…"

"I would be delighted to." Pulling out a chair at the table, Mark sat and smiled as Ava hurriedly planted her butt on the chair beside him.

"Good. Can you tell me all about what it's like to be in the movies?" she gushed.

Abbi knelt to get paper plates from under the counter. A frown working its way onto her forehead. She knew Ben had to leave soon. But she wished it wasn't this soon. She felt like staying right down there on the floor, to sit and have a good cry, when she noticed two feet standing beside her.

Slowly she looked up, seeing an offered hand.

"Let me take those for you." Ben gave her hand a light squeeze before taking the plates to the table. He piled a plate with pizza and walked to the fridge, grabbing a pop that he tucked under his arm.

He took Abbi by the hand and led her through the living room to the back porch. Putting the food and drink on the table, he took her into his arms. "I don't want to leave yet," he murmured. "Not now, maybe never."

"It's okay, Ben. I know you have a job to do. It's a couple of weeks away. Let's not think about it till then. Who knows? Maybe it will be delayed again." She leaned back, looking into his eyes. Ben saw her eyes glisten with unshed tears that nearly tore his heart out.

He nodded, despite knowing that wouldn't happen. "Right, you're right." He sighed heavily, "Let's eat, shall we?"

They sat down, digging into the food, each lost in their thoughts. If Mark didn't have any useful information for him, Ben would find a way to stay here, or bring Abbi along. Tony wouldn't like that. He found it distracting for the actors when friends and family were milling about. But Tony could hardly refuse the author from attending the set. Ben bit into a slice of pizza and decided that's exactly what he'd do.

"Say, Abbi, when was the last time you went on a holiday?"

"Hmm, let me think… Oh, I know. Never," she said, chuckling.

Stunned, he looked at her, "What! How could you not?"

"I don't like traveling."

He took a swig of the pop. "I see…" Well, he could understand that. He rather hated it himself.

"Why? Were you thinking of taking me with you?"

"The thought crossed my mind." He brushed the crumbs from his hands.

"Maybe... For you I'll let my guard down this once," she laughed.

"You would? For me?"

Abbi nodded.

"It's settled. When the time comes, you're coming with me." He leaned over giving a quick kiss to her lips.

"Wait. Filming is where, right now?" Abbi frowned.

He wiped his mouth. "Madrid, Spain." He glanced at her, noticing the frown. "Why?"

She sighed already feeling anxious. "Well, I best be drunk or drugged.... I don't do planes," she laughed apprehensively.

He raised his brows. "Seriously?"

"Ah... Yup. Maybe I'll just stay here?"

"No way, we sealed it with a kiss, remember?" he teased. He'd never make her do anything she didn't want to.

She remembered. How could she forget those lips? Damn it! Fine, she'd go. She held her hands up in defeat. "I know, I know! I'll go. But be forewarned. If I go a little crazy, don't blame me."

"Deal," he smiled. "You do realize I would never make you do anything you didn't want to, right?"

"I know, Ben. I know," she smiled.

Ava and Mark came out onto the porch just then, in a flurry of giggles. "Hey, guys. We are just going for a walk along the shore for a bit." Ava looked towards the lake.

"Um, okay," Abbi answered, a look of concern on her face. "Don't be too long, if you can help it. The guys should set up the fireworks shortly." She wanted to say 'Hell no! You aren't going anywhere with Mark'. She had to bite her lip from speaking her mind. Ava was an adult. Abbi had no right to tell her what she could and could not do any longer.

Ben noted the worry on Abbi's face as she watched them walk away. "Love don't worry. Mark isn't that stupid. Besides, he respects you too much."

"Mhm, let's hope not," she replied, distractedly.

Lane and Luke came from the side of the house, the dogs in tow. "We're going to set up the fireworks," Lane said waving one in the air.

"It's going to be a killer show this year. We spent over two grand on them," Luke added.

"Nice! If you need a hand, just yell," Ben offered.

"Sure thing," Luke nodded.

Kim ambled out onto the porch, followed by Greg and Nancy. She jerked a thumb towards the house. "The drug store dropped off a bag for you, Ben. And Abbi, some flowers were in the middle of your laneway. The delivery driver brought them up to the house." She wrinkled her nose in distaste.

"Flowers?" Abbi and Ben both asked, equally shocked. Puzzlement etched across Abbi's face, while Ben's showed a murderous look.

Kim noticed immediately that Ben was glaring at her. "Hey, don't shoot the messenger. If it's any consolation, it looks like they were trampled on a few times," she said defensively.

"It's not you Kim, that I'm pissed with." Getting up, Ben stalked into the house, followed quickly by Abbi.

Hurrying behind him, Abbi plowed into his back when he abruptly stopped before the table. Holding onto his arms to steady herself, she peeked around him. There in the middle of the dining room table was a dozen long-stemmed roses, thorns and all, laying on a newspaper. Kim had been right. The once beautiful petals were bruised and crushed. They looked as if they were weeping... blood? There was an envelope lying in the middle, nestled among the leaves.

Ben looked at Abbi, a foreboding furrow on his brow. He stepped closer to the table. Reaching out, he went to take the envelope.

Should I touch it, or should I call the police? ... To hell with it, it may be nothing. Maybe the wind had just blown them into Abbi's yard. He snatched the envelope and tore it open. Abbi waited with bated breath.

"Son of a bitch!!" Ben yelled. Running his hand through his hair, he started to pace the floor.

"What!" Abbi cried in alarm. "What is it?"

He cast a soft look in her direction. "Abbi no. You're not seeing this." He had to protect her at all costs and the first way to do that was protecting her emotions.

She held out her hand. "Ben. Let me see it."

Mechanically, he watched his own hands as he folded the note.

Shaking his head, he looked at her. "No, I'm sorry. I can't do that. This is something that doesn't concern you... yet." He stuffed the paper in his pocket. He had to get Mark back here now and find out exactly what his brother told him.

"Yet? What does that even mean?" She spat the words out.

"I'll let you know, when I know."

"Fine, be stubborn." She turned on her heel, marching outside.

Ben let her go. He had to. Otherwise, he would have given in... showing her the note. He carefully rolled the newspaper around the flowers. He needed to get rid of them before she came back. Opening the front door, he closed it behind him with a soft thud. Looking around, he figured the weeds were as good a place as any and stalked across the front yard, crossing the road. He tossed them in the brush along the road. Standing there with his hands on his hips, he turned, looking at her house. No, he did the right thing.

He had to talk to Mark now, taking out his cell, he dialed Mark's number.

Waiting for the call to connect, his thoughts turned to Abbi. If she had seen it, she'd be a basket case at this very moment if he had given in. How else would she have reacted if she had read those words? Words that looked like they were etched in blood. Five simple words… *I'm coming for you Abbi…*.

Chapter 6

It was a beautiful night for a walk. The water was gently lapping on the shoreline; gulls were flying back and forth. Damn, Mark was kicking himself again, for selling to Ben. He had been a fool, staying away from such a beautiful place all the years he'd owned it.

"So, how do you like living so far away from your mother?" he asked Ava.

"I hate it. We only get to see each other a couple of times a year now. Like I understand why she wanted to leave home, but damn… so far away is hard, you know?"

"Yeah, I can understand that," Mark nodded.

After the initial shock wore off from meeting him and realizing Ben was also a famous actor, more so than he, Ava had turned out to be cool. He was amazed at how much he liked her. *What is it with the Peterson woman?* It was like they were witches or something. Bewitching everyone they met. He shook his head, bewilderment.

He glanced out at the lake, noticing a boat not too far from shore. 'Pearl Lake Yacht and Boat Rentals' was written on the side. "I didn't know you could rent boats like that around here," he nodded towards the lake.

Ava glanced at where he was looking. "Yeah, only recently though. Like in the last year or so."

"Maybe I'll check it out while I'm here. When are you heading back home?" he asked.

"Well, I haven't mentioned it to Mom yet, we've been so busy. But I have the next two weeks off. Now I'm not sure I'll say anything though… with Ben being here and all." She wrinkled her nose.

"Why not?" he asked.

"Well, you know, I don't want to be in the way. Say, do you think Ben is serious about her?" she asked. "I… Never mind. Forget I asked that. It must be against the man code, bros before hoes, to discuss things like that."

Mark stopped. He grabbed the sleeve of her jacket, stopping her in her tracks. "Honestly, it's fine," he smiled. "I've known Ben for a few years now, and I know he'd expect me to answer you. He's just that kind of guy." He paused, thinking his words over carefully. *How much does she already know?*

"Yeah, well like I said, we have known each other for a while. I met him around the time he and his ex split. He made a promise to himself, never to take any relationship for granted, ever. Which he never did, but you know some woman, if you're not in their face 24/7 they feel neglected," he said, glancing at her. "Erm… um. Sorry got carried away there for a minute," he chuckled. "Anyway, he wanted to make sure the next one he had would be his last."

"Just spit it out will you," Ava said.

"I'm getting to it, gee will you relax?" He laughed. He loved her spunk. "Yes, he's serious about her. If he weren't, he wouldn't be here. I can guarantee that." He started walking again. "He's had women falling at his feet. Beautiful, gorgeous, stunning woman. And do you know what he does?"

She shook her head.

"He steps right over them and keeps walking."

"Well, that's a dick move if I ever heard one," Ava said, frowning.

"No, you don't get it. These women pounce on him if he stops. Hell, some even grab his…. Ah… well, you know!" Mark said, nodding, his brows raised.

Her brows shot up in response. "Oh! I see. Um… Well, it makes perfect sense then." She looked at the boat again. It was only fifty feet from them now. She shielded her eyes, trying to make out the person at the helm. They looked familiar but she couldn't put her finger on it for the life of her. She waved, but they were so intent on watching… the house.

Mark stopped, pulling his cell from his back pocket. "It's Ben." He hit the talk button. "Hey Buddy, what's up?" he wrinkled his brow as he ran the tip of his tongue back and forth across his bottom lip. "What? No, no, there wasn't anything like that when I came over." Mark glanced at Ava, frowning, "Yeah, we will be right there in…" he gave Ava a questioning look, she held up one hand, "… five minutes. Yep, we'll be quick, we can see the house from here…. M'kay… Bye."

"What was that about?" Ava asked, a sudden chill causing her to stuff her hands in her pockets, oddly enough the breeze was warm.

"Well, your mom is pissed at Ben and someone left some flowers in the driveway, dead ones, with an apparent nasty note. Come on. I have to talk to Ben."

"You were just talking to him," Ava pointed out.

"Yeah, but in private."

"You could have just told me to walk ahead, you know," she said testily. "And why is she pissed at Ben?"

"Will you just clam it for once and hurry it up," he laughed to soften his words.

"Sure, race you there," she took off at a jog. Mark shook his head as her laughter carried in the wind.

The boat floated soundlessly on the still waters of Pearl Lake. It was soothing really. One day, they would live just a few hundred yards from where the boat now sat. They lowered the binoculars slowly. Interesting. Very interesting... So, Ben, you didn't like the little present I left for MY Abbi? How dare he touch them! And to throw them into the brush as if they meant nothing...as if they were trash! They hoped that Abbi was able to see them before that bastard removed them from the house. Ah, no worries. He will soon be out of the way... very soon, indeed.

A feeling of pure elation coursed through their veins. Knowing that in less than 48 hours, when her family was heading back home, she'd be free, free of her family, free of his parents, but more importantly free from Ben Quinn.... forever...

Turning the helm, they directed the boat back towards its base. They would wait...It would be all over the news in no time that the great Hollywood actor was found dead.

Ben hung up the phone; he had to find Abbi. Tell her how sorry he was before Mark and Ava returned. Jogging across the front yard, he ran alongside the house. He stopped, looking on the porch to find it empty. Glancing down towards the lake, he saw her sitting there with his mum and Kim. His dad was helping Luke and Lane set up the fireworks. He walked up to them, stopping short of the back of Abbi's chair. Mark and Ava were still not there.

"Hey, buddy," Kim called to him. "Why don't you sit," she said, half-standing to offer him her seat.

He saw Abbi tense. "No, you stay there. I'll just sit over there," he said. Crossing the circle around the fire pit, he took the seat directly across from Abbi.

"Alright, I'll just start a fire then. So, what's new with you?" Kim asked, glancing at Ben while she piled logs in the pit.

Kim felt terrible about the flowers. She should have just thrown them away; they were hideous. And even if they weren't, no one ever sent her sister flowers. So, was someone trying to cause trouble between them? But who, if that was the case? As far as she knew, only the people here knew that Abbi and Ben were in a relationship.

Ben cleared his throat before answering Kim. "Nothing much," he sighed, staring at Abbi. She wouldn't even glance his way. Just kept talking to his mother as if he wasn't even there.

"Mum, when are you and dad heading back to England?"

"Oh, I was just telling Abbi here, that we have decided to travel a bit. Head towards Montreal or the East Coast, perhaps. Oh, I have the most brilliant idea! Why don't you and Ben come with us, dear?" She smiled, her face lighting up as she laid a hand on Abbi's knee. She sent a wink to her son.

You sly woman... Ben flashed his mum a smile of thanks.

"Ah, uh…" Abbi looked at Ben, a smile on her face. She remembered just then that she was still mad at him. Furrowing her brow, she gave him a dirty look and turned to his mother. "Thank you for the invite Nancy, it is sweet of you. But I must decline. I'm afraid I've put my book on hold long enough. I really need to get it done. Ben might tag along with you though." She smiled sweetly in his direction.

He rose his brows in shock; she really was pissed at him. Well enough of that, he decided. He got up and crossed the circle. Standing before her, he scooped her up and tossed her onto his shoulder. She screamed, of course, to be put down… NOW! But he didn't… he carried her off towards the house as she pummeled his back with her hands. With all her squirming, he was losing his grip on her. Moving his hand, he tucked it in between her legs, accidentally grazing her warmth.

"Oh, my!" She gasped as the fight fled her.

He stopped, setting her on the porch steps.

"That was so unfair just so you know," she muttered.

"I'm sorry. I never intended to do that; you were slipping. I just grabbed," he mumbled apologetically, touching her face.

"Abbi, I'm sorry... for everything. I shouldn't have withheld that note from you," he said looking away. "But I had a very good reason to. I did it to protect you. But I realized this is something you need to know."

"You could have let me be the judge of that, you know."

"I know, I just didn't think. I reacted, okay? Forgive me, please?" he raised his eyes to her.

Nodding, she was interrupted from answering, as Mark and Ava ran up to them out of breath.

"Whew! Man, am I out of shape." Mark bent over, sucking air into his lungs.

Ava poked him in the ribs. "That's cuz you're not used to outrunning girls," she laughed.

"No, no, you're right! But I won, didn't I?" He wheezed.

"Ha! I let you win."

"I hate to interrupt your exchange here," Ben said, motioning back and forth with his hand. "But we need to talk, Mark... *now!*"

He looked at Abbi taking her hand. Feeling her chilled skin, he took a blanket from the nearby chair and draped it over her shoulders. "No more secrets. Come on. The rest of the family needs to hear this as well," he said.

"What's going on, Mom?"

"I have no idea," Abbi answered, as Ben guided her to the lake. "Come on, baby girl, we're about to find out."

"Lane, Luke, Dad. Can you come to the fire please," Ben called to them.

Everyone took a seat, waiting for Ben to tell them all what was so important.

"There has been some… strange things happening around here lately. Before you all arrived." His eyes settled on Abbi's face. Everyone present could see he was in love with her. "Abbi has been getting calls from an unknown number for, how long?" he asked, looking at her.

She shrugged. "Oh, I don't know, for about six months or so."

"Six months?" Ben looked at her in amazement. He wondered exactly what else had been happening before he had arrived.

Abbi squirmed like a bug under a microscope. "What? … It happens."

Looking at her with exasperation, he couldn't believe how trusting and naïve she was.

"Right…" he glanced around at everyone. "Aside from that. She's heard laughter and music. Coming from what she thought was my house. Thinking it was me when I was likely asleep, as I had just arrived from England."

"Okay, so what does all of this mean?" Lane asked.

"At first, I thought the paparazzi had found out I was living here. I became convinced the more things happened the more it wasn't me they were after." His mouth was set in a grim line.

"Last week, there was blood on my porch, a lot of it. That night, coming back from the clinic, Abbi was driving and almost hit Molly who was sitting in the middle of the road." He nodded to the dogs lying flat out on the lawn.

"Oh, my goodness!" Nancy cried out, covering her mouth as the image played through her mind.

Greg reached out a hand, patting her leg.

"She was in bad shape, dirty and bloody. We took her to Mack, he patched her up and gave her some meds.

But he determined the gash on her side was from a scalpel."

"What?!" Mark exclaimed.

"Yeah," Ben nodded.

"What kind of sicko would do such a thing?" Luke asked, a look of disgust crossing his face.

"A dangerous one," Lane supplied.

"After that, I surmised, they were trying to warn me off." Ben glanced at Abbi. "That will never happen," he softly told her. "I asked Abbi what had happened to the person who had been stalking her before."

"What did happen to him, Abbi?" Kim asked.

"I went to the police and had a restraining order put on him. After that, I moved here, and I never heard from him again," she said shakily.

Ben saw she was on the verge of losing it again. He wanted to pull her over to him and sit her in his lap. But he didn't. Instead, he got up and sat on the ground at her feet. She parted her legs, allowing him to rest his back against the seat of her chair. He felt her place a hand on his shoulder. Reaching up, he held it in his, tracing circles on her palm.

"Until now," Mark piped up. "Ben called me a few days ago, Tuesday, wasn't it?" Mark looked at him for confirmation.

"That's right," Ben said nodding. He laid his head back looking up at Abbi. "I went on your computer and found his name," he said, gazing into her eyes. "I'm sorry about that."

She answered him with a watery smile. She leaned forward, kissing him softly, as tears fell from her eyes.

Mark cleared his throat. "Ahem….?"

They both looked at him. His eyes were large as silver dollars as he stared at them. "As I was saying…" He rolled his eyes. "Ben called me, giving me as much info as he could from your files,

Abbi. My brother is a cop. He worked his magic and found that your stalker left his last known address years ago. Ah, there was a hit a month ago." Mark scratched his head, "The cops pulled him over in Springbank. Now, there is no guarantee that this is Jacob Randal, but it is a possibility," he sighed.

"What did your brother suggest we do?" Greg asked.

"He said that she could get another restraining order. But needs proof that it is him. His current address is in Ottawa, that's a fair distance from here. I'm having my doubts, that it's him," Mark said.

"To be honest… I have to agree with Mark," Abbi said. She could feel Ben move uncomfortably against her. "I say that only because the pattern is different. This time, this person seems… I don't know, sneakier." She paused, she had to tell them. "Jacob was never afraid of telling me what he wanted to do with me. He sent me flowers and gifts. This person almost seems more…. calculating…." she trailed off.

"Okay mom, I get where you're coming from, but who else could it be?" Ava asked, concern etching her brow.

"I don't know, maybe a local?" Abbi said. She motioned a hand towards the water's edge. "Someone who is bold enough to sit not a hundred feet from the shore."

Ben added, "Someone who is brazen enough to walk in this yard, and leave mashed up flowers with a note." He didn't want to say what was on that note. "Someone who knows their way around a boat," he said instead.

"Boat you say?" Mark asked.

Ben nodded.

Mark was thinking about the boat he and Ava saw on their walk. "Guys. Was there writing on that boat?"

"There was, wasn't there?" Ben looked up at Abbi.

Nodding, she tried to picture it in her mind. "Yes. I just can't remember what it said, now."

Ava knew where Mark was going with his line of questioning. "Was it, Pearl Lake Yacht and Boat Rentals, by chance?" she asked.

"Yes! That's it," they said in unison.

"How did you know?" Ben asked.

"On our walk earlier. There was a boat not more than 50 feet from shore," Ava said pausing. "I thought I recognized the person, I even waved, but they were too busy looking off…"

"Looking off at what Ava…?" Ben questioned, already feeling he had the answer.

"The house," Mark supplied. "He was looking at this house."

Chapter 7

A hushed silence fell over everyone sitting before the fire, each one lost in their thoughts. Abbi moved her legs from either side of Ben. Getting up, she immediately settled herself on the ground beside him, sharing her blanket with him.

"Come here, my love," he said, tucking her close beside him. He could feel her shivering against his body as he brushed his lips against her temple.

"But what did the note say?" Greg asked. Ben closed his eyes. *Thanks, dad, I didn't want to say it!*

Taking a deep breath, he whispered, "Move here, love." He patted the ground between his legs. Before he said anything, he wanted to make sure she was in the safety of his arms, He wrapped the blanket around them both, enveloping her in his warmth "Okay?" he asked her. At her nod, he began. "The note said five words… five words that looked like they were written in blood."

Ben felt her body tense from head to toe. He brought her closer to his chest. "It said… I'm coming for you, Abbi…"

His mother gasped while everyone else swore, everyone except Abbi. She just trembled in his embrace. He hugged her to him tighter.

"I didn't want to tell you, you know that, right?" he whispered.

She nodded, hugging him tightly. "It's okay. It's better to know and expect something to happen than be oblivious," she whispered against his neck. *Thank God he had me move down here with him.* If he hadn't, she'd have shot out of her chair, running blindly, screaming her fool head off.

He was her protector. He was her haven against all storms; she realized that now.

She trusted him more than she'd ever trusted anyone in her entire life.

The loons suddenly made their nightly appearance. Hauntingly calling out their song, it somehow seemed fitting to Abbi. For at that very moment, all she wanted to do was cry along with them.

"Well, now that that's all out in the open, why don't we forget about all of this until tomorrow and have a hell of a good time," Kim stated, standing up.

Ava took her cue. "Sounds like a plan to me. Let's get the booze Aunt Kim," she said, looping arms with her aunt. "Mark, give us a hand, will ya?" Ava asked, nodding at him.

Rubbing his hands together, he sprung up out of his chair. "Absolutely!" He followed them to the house. All three of them ready to have their spirits lifted.

Luke and Lane went back to setting up the fireworks; they needed to work fast, before the dark settled in.

Nancy and Greg decided they would sit on the porch to watch the show. They called for the dogs, taking them with them as they headed towards the house.

"Hey dad, can you make sure you shut the dogs in, please? Don't want them running scared from the noise," Ben called after them.

"Right! Will do son," Greg responded, giving him a slight smile. Ben nodded his thanks.

Abbi hadn't moved a muscle since he revealed the contents of the note. He gave her a gentle squeeze. "How you are doing, love?" he asked.

She tilted her head up to meet his gaze, looking him straight in the eyes, she failed at giving him a reassuring smile. "Like shit."

He chuckled at her honesty. "You don't feel like shit. You feel damn good right about now." He said, turning her to face him.

She leaned her forehead on his. "I don't know what I would do without you in my life. Until I met you, I was merely existing. No matter what happens, please know that you are so, so very important to me and you always will be." Her voice cracked on the last word. She needed to feel alive because at this very moment she felt like a shell of a person. She kissed him softly, her tears threatening to spill at any moment.

He broke off the kiss, taking her face in his hands, he searched her eyes. "Love…. Please don't talk like that. Don't think something will happen, okay?"

Tears welled in the corners of her eyes. Slipping slowly down her cheeks, she quickly brushed them away to no avail.

"Abbi, I'm serious."

She looked away.

"No, don't do that. Look at me." He gently wiped her tears away. "I will be here for you, always. I would go to the ends of the earth for you. You know that don't you?" he asked softly.

She shrugged. She knew nothing anymore.

He licked his lips. He was nervous as hell. "Abbi, you own my heart. Do you understand what I'm trying to say to you?" he asked gently.

She looked at him then, her lashes spiked from crying, she wiped them with her sleeves.

"I'm in love with you, Abbi."

She stopped mid-swipe. *Did I hear him correctly?*

Her brows shot so high they almost disappeared into her hair. She blinked rapidly. "Come again?"

He chuckled. "I said…I'm in love with you. More than I love the very air that I breathe," he murmured.

"Are you sure?" she asked hesitantly.

"Right!" He pursed his lips. "Was it too soon?" He nodded his head vigorously, "I said it too soon, didn't I?" He felt like an idiot.

Suddenly she was blubbering like a fool, her tears streamed down her face, snot bubbles formed at her nose. *What the hell is wrong with me?...* She cried uncontrollably. She risked a glance through the wave of tears, half expecting him to set her aside, a disgusted look on his face and get up leaving her to sit and wallow in the dirt, alone.

Ben just sat there with a confused look on his handsome face. *What the hell did I do now?* He didn't know whether to join her in crying or laugh his ass off at her. He thought it might be better if he just offered her his sleeve. "Here love, use this." He held out his arm.

"No. I can't," she squeaked, shaking her head. She sobbed, "I'll get snot all over your sweater."

He smiled and shrugged his shoulders. "Meh. It's fine, I can wash it," he said indifferently.

She wiped her face on the back of his sleeve; runny nose and all. She heaved a heavy sigh. "I don't know what it is about you. But you have a knack for making me cry," she chuckled.

"Don't forget blushing too."

"Yeah, that too," she smiled.

Feeling awkward now, he returned her smile. "So, yeah... do you feel any better?" he asked. He didn't dare mention the word love to her again. She likely would fill the lake with her tears if he did.

In response, she wrapped her arms around his neck, planting a kiss on his mouth.

A groan escaped from the depths of his throat. She was put on this earth to drive him insane; he'd finally come to that conclusion.

He deepened the kiss as he held her face in his hand. It felt so long since they had kissed this way. It was only a day or so but felt like an eternity since he had tasted her sweet lips.

Pulling away from him, she murmured, "No, you didn't say it too soon. You said it at the perfect time." She saw the relief wash over his face.

"Do you mean…?" It scared him to say the rest of it.

Reaching out a hand she touched his lips, tracing the curve of his mouth with a finger. She gazed into his eyes, eyes that showed him how much she loved him. The moment he saw it, his own darkened in response.

She nodded.

He covered her mouth with his, drinking in her sweetness. If their families weren't there at that very moment, he would have laid her on the ground in front of the fire. He had to stop before it went that far. Breathing heavily, Abbi said the words he so longed to hear.

"I'm in love with you, Ben. I think I was the moment you caught me in Mack's," she smiled, remembering back to that day. "At first I thought you were an ass."

He laughed at her admission. "What? Why would you think that?"

"Have you looked at yourself in the mirror? Guys that look like you, are generally assholes… just saying," she said.

"I don't know how to feel about that," he replied in shock.

"It's not how you look, but what you look like," Abbi explained.

"Gotcha," he said. Pursing his lips, he gave her a wink.

"Would you really go to the ends of the earth for me?" she asked, wanting to know.

"Absolutely, without a doubt. Abbi, I would do anything for you. If you want me to quit acting, just say so."

She was stunned. She couldn't believe he'd even suggest that. "No. I could never ask that of anyone. That's your career, your life," she said, shaking her head.

"I too thought that myself once... until I moved here. I fell in love with the area right away. But it will always be here waiting for me to go back, just like England, you know?"

She laid her head on his chest, loving the sound of his voice resonating within.

"And then one day I woke up, and I realized..." he paused, lifting her chin for her to look at him. "What's keeping my heart here is you. I mean it... just say the word, and I'm done." He looked at her with such sincerity; she knew he meant it.

They could hear Mark and the girls approaching from behind them, stopping them from discussing anything further. Abbi reluctantly pulled herself up from the comfort of Ben's arms. Standing, she offered him a hand up; she noticed him wincing in pain when he put his weight on his arm.

"Ben are you okay?" she asked, concerned.

"Yeah, just a little stiff is all." Honestly, it was more than just a little stiff. It was hurting like the day he had injured it. But he refused to admit it; she was worried about enough already. He didn't need to add to it.

She knew it was more than that, she could tell by the look on his face. "I'll go get those meds that Doc dropped off."

"No. I'm fine. Just need to loosen it up a bit." He said, rotating his shoulder in circles.

"I don't like taking anything stronger than what I have been." He needed his wits about him; he'd be of no use to anyone, especially Abbi if he was flat on his ass.

"I can just cut one in half?" she said, laying her hand on his forearm.

He couldn't deny her any longer, stroking her cheek. He leaned down, giving her a quick kiss. "Alright, love, for you. But only half."

Nodding, Abbi said, "I'll be right back." Pivoting on her heel, she ran off to the house.

"So, Ben. What are we going to do about this creep hanging around?" Kim looked at him, her eyes full of worry.

"Well, I for one, am staying here until they catch this guy. I've already called the shop and told them I'll be off for a bit and left Marissa in charge," Ava said.

Mark looked at her. "Wait... what do you do again?"

"I already told you... don't you listen? I own a spa... remember?"

"Oh yeah! Well, it was kind of hard to listen when your hands were all over me." Mark looked at her like the rake he was.

Ben let out a bark of laughter. "Whoa!!! What were you two doing?" he grinned, looking between the two of them.

"Ava! What the hell?" Kim chimed in.

"Massage people; I gave him a massage." She threw a hand in Mark's direction. "This fool thought he could do a somersault and twisted the wrong way."

Ben shook his head, grinning. "Man, some things never change with you, do they?"

"Never, Benny boy, never!"

"Hey, guys you about ready for the fireworks?" Lane asked joining them.

"Yeah," Ben said, looking around.

He had that feeling someone was watching again. He looked out across the lake. Distractedly, he said to Lane, "Your mom just ran into the house for a minute."

A hint of light directly across from where he stood caught his attention. Not a light but more of a quick flash or a... *reflection?*

"Perfect. Gives us enough time to finish up." Lane turned, yelling as he walked to relay the message to Luke.

Abbi went out onto the porch. Stopping, she looked at Nancy and Greg.

"Are you two okay up here?" she asked, laying a hand on Greg's shoulder.

"Oh yes, dear! It's the perfect spot!" Nancy answered, nestling into the blanket wrapped around her.

"Great, if you need anything, please help yourself to whatever is in the house. I'm just going to run this down to Ben." She held out her hand to show them the pill. "His shoulder is giving him a bit of trouble tonight." With a wave, she went down the steps, sprinting to the lake.

Nancy and Greg watched as she went. "I like her, don't you?" Greg glanced at his wife. Her stamp of approval was pivotal in their relationship with their son; he knew Ben would choose Abbi over them any day.

"Mhm," Nancy paused, looking over at Greg. "He couldn't have done better if I had picked her myself," she said grinning while she took his hand.

Ben turned when he felt a hand run down his back.

"Here you go handsome," Abbi said, smiling as she held out her hand to him.

"Oh, almost forgot." She dug a bottle of water out of her jacket pocket, handing that over, too.

"Thanks love," he said, popping the pill into his mouth,

followed with a swig of water to wash it down.

"What were you looking at out there?" Abbi asked with a nod towards the dark lake.

"Ah... nothing. The guys are ready to set the fireworks off." Ben motioned down towards the shore with the water bottle.

"Oh good! I can't wait," Abbi smiled, taking the chair next to Kim.

Ben sat down on the ground once again in front of Abbi. He took her ankles, bringing them around his waist, he set to work massaging her calf muscles. He could feel her relaxing under his touch.

Kim nudged Abbi with her elbow, motioning for Abbi to come closer. Leaning towards her she whispered in her ear, "I'm thrilled for you. I'll be honest at first I thought you were robbing the cradle." She held up a staying hand. "I know, I know! That's not your style, and you battled your demons to get to this point. But after getting to know his parents and Ben and the way he is with you; I see that it's for real. I just wanted to tell you that." Her eyes sparkled softly in the glow from the fire.

Abbi wrapped her arms around Kim. "Thank you... I love you, sis," she whispered.

Kim returned the hug and leaned back, looking into her eyes. "I love you too, baby girl." She waved her hand and wiped her eyes. "Now enough of this wishy-washy shit." Both broke out in a burst of hysterical laughter, tears streaming down they faces.

Smiling, Ben laid his head back in Abbi's lap, looking up at the two of them as he rubbed her thigh, "What are you two going on about now?"

Leaning forward, she ran a finger across his bottom lip. Her lips followed with a soft lingering kiss. Oh, how she loved them...

loved him. She lifted her head, looking into his eyes.

"Nothing, just girl talk," she smiled. "I love you," she added softly.

"I love you more," he said, with a dreamy look in his eyes.

"Not likely," Abbi muttered under her breath.

A small smile graced his lips at hearing her words.

She noticed how tired he looked as she took his hand in hers, thinking how cold it felt.

The first burst of fireworks lit the night sky catching Abbi's attention. They watched in awe as one after another danced and soared high above the lake, falling in shimmery trails onto the mirrored surface.

Abbi felt Ben's hand go limp. *That's odd, there is no way he can sleep with all this noise....* She peered down at him, running a hand along his jawline. "Hey sleepyhead," she said as the next set of fireworks zoomed into the night sky, lighting his face. "Ben?" she said, placing both hands alongside his face. Panic set in. She nudged him, "Ben! ... Ben!" Tears sprang to her eyes, running down her cheeks, splashing his face. "Please God, wake him up!" she pleaded, placing a shaky hand on his neck. Feeling a slow but steady heartbeat, "KIM!!! Help him!!" she cried in alarm.

Kim looked down to see what Abbi was talking about. One look was all it took. "Oh, shit!" Jumping up, she told Abbi to move back as she bent down in front of Ben.

Ava and Mark looked over to see what the commotion was.

"Ava! Call Doc, NOW!" Kim ordered.

"Mark! Luke! Lane! Come help me move Ben. We need to lay him down," she yelled.

Abbi scurried over taking his hand as they laid him gently on his back. Kim checked his pulse while glancing at his chest to see the slow rise and fall of it. "He's breathing. Does anyone have a flashlight?"

"Here," Mark said holding his phone out for her.

Kim checked his pupils to see if they were fixed. They were damn it! Checking to see if there was anything in his mouth, she then stuck her finger in to check his throat.

Abbi dashed away the blinding tears, watching as Kim turned Ben on his side.

"Abbi, run to the house and ask his parents if he's allergic to anything." She glanced up to see Abbi frozen. "Abbi, snap out of it!" Kim reached out and smacked her across the face. That got her attention. "Get up to the house and ask his mom if he's allergic to anything."

Abbi bobbed her head up and down. "Yes, yes, I can do that," she got up. She had to tear her gaze from Ben, not wanting to leave him. She wanted to curl up beside him, hold him tight and tell him everything would be okay... like he did for her so many times before. Turning, she ran as fast as she could to the house. She flew up the steps, alarming his parents. "Ben has had some kind of reaction, is he allergic to anything?" Abbi panted, trying desperately to sound as calm as she could.

Nancy stood up in horror. "Oh my Lord, where is he?" She hurried down the steps.

Greg took Abbi by the arms. "No, he isn't allergic to anything. Come on, let's go," he said in a worried voice.

Abbi took off running back to Ben, passing by Nancy, not stopping to wait for her. Her only focus was to get back to him. Abbi knelt by his side, taking his hand.

"What's wrong with him?" Ava asked.

"Well, I'm only a nurse. But I would say he's been drugged,"

Kim answered.

"That can't be," Abbi found her voice. "He hates taking any drugs, he didn't even want to take over-the-counter medication."

Nancy and Greg came up with Doc just then.

"Hey, Doc," Kim called out.

"Hi, Kim. What's the prognosis?" he asked. Kneeling beside Ben, Doc put on his stethoscope. He held a hand up, signaling for silence. Finding his beat to be slow but steady, Doc looked up to Kim, nodding for her to continue as he checked his eyes.

"His breathing is shallow; his heartbeat was slow but steady. Pupils are fixed," she looked at Doc. "If I didn't know any better, I would say he's been..."

"Drugged," Doc said, finishing for her.

"Yes! But he didn't take anything, did he?" she said, looking to Abbi.

Abbi started to shake her head. A horrified look flashed across her face. "Yes. His shoulder was hurting him earlier. Just before the fireworks." Tears were dripping from her eyes at the memory of him not wanting to take it but caving in for her.

Doc turned around to face Abbi. "What did he take, Abbi? The pharmacy said he never picked up the script I sent you home with," he said.

"I gave him a half of a pill. The ones you had delivered earlier today. The directions said to take two, but he didn't want any," she answered. Her face crumpled as she laid a hand on Ben's chest. She needed to feel him, to touch him.

Doc reached over Ben, taking her by the arms, he gave her a shake. "Where are those pills now, Abbi?" he asked with urgency.

"They're in the house."

"I need to take them with me for testing." A look of concern crossed his face as he glanced down at Ben again.

Making a judgment call with no time to waste, Doc took a vial of Naloxone and a syringe out of his bag. Measuring the amount, he jabbed the needle in Ben's arm, jamming the plunger down.

"Why would you need to test them?" Luke asked.

"Because when Ben didn't pick up the initial prescription, I didn't bother getting the ones from Springbank brought in."

"So they must have had them in stock after all?" Greg asked.

"On the contrary. They don't." Doc gave his full attention back to Abbi. "I never wrote another prescription for Ben, Abbi. And I sent no one out here to deliver them. Whoever did this... I suspect, they were targeting Ben."

Abbi shook her head in denial; it just can't be. *Who would do such a thing...?* With dawning horror, she knew Doc was right. She now knew that Ben was right all along. A low keening started in her throat as she collapsed on him, hugging him to her. Willing him to wake up.

Abbi sat back on her haunches and looked up to the heavens, tears streaming down her face. "Nooooooo!!!" her wailing screams could be heard echoing over the stillness of the lake.

"Luke, Lane, you," he pointed to Mark. "I'll need help to get him out to my van," Doc called out

"Where will you be taking him?" Nancy asked, her voice thick with worry.

"I'll be watching him at the clinic tonight," Doc said, looking up at her.

All four men picked up Ben gently. Hurriedly, they started across the long expanse of the yard.

Over his shoulder, Doc called out, "Kim, Ava. Get Abbi to my van, now! She needs to be with him, and someone grab those pills!"

Perfect.... My plan was a success, I see! Lowering the binoculars, a bubble of pure glee erupted from their throat as the wailing cries of their dear sweet Abbi, rang out over the lake. Directly across was the perfect place, a front-row seat...so to speak. Clapping, they silently congratulated Ben Quinn on his stellar performance... his last one. A shame the world couldn't have seen it. Oh! Abbi darling, soon I will comfort you, holding you in MY arms! Just a few more days and your house will be empty, as will your heart. I will fill that hole... I promise you that my dear!

Chapter 8

Abbi had never felt so alone in her life, standing alone by Ben's bed. Both of their families had come. His mother, only leaving when she knew her son would pull through.

Abbi reached out to brush the hair from his forehead. Bending down, she placed a quivering kiss on his brow. It pained her so, knowing what she had to do. But she had made her mind up.

A gentle squeeze on her shoulder had her straightening. Turning, she saw Doc standing there, concern for her, filling his eyes. "Abbi, I'll bring you a cot. You need to get some sleep," he said, as he quietly left the room.

She nodded numbly. There were no tears left. Fighting with her own emotions, she had cried a river's worth of tears. Now all she felt was an emptiness and the greatest loss of her life. She let out a heavy sigh. Taking Ben's hand, she held it softly, running her thumb across the back. Memorizing each vein that stood out on his soft skin. Knowing in her heart it would be the last time she did. She listened as the machine beeped with every beat of his heart.

He was also hooked up to an IV. He was stable. He just needed to wake up Doc told her. The lab tests would take time to come back, he'd said, but he was confident that it was a drug of sorts that put Ben into this state. Lucky for him, he hadn't taken the full amount; otherwise, it would have affected his liver or kidneys or worse... She shuddered at the thought.

"Here Abbi." Doc said, rolling a fold-up bed into the room. "It's not the best thing, but it's more comfortable than the chair."

"Thanks, Doc," she mumbled.

"Abbi. He will be fine. He's young... he's healthy and strong. He just needs to sleep it off," he told her, trying to ease her fears. "If I didn't think he would be, I would have called for the air ambulance back at your place."

"I know. I just feel like it's my fault. If I hadn't persisted that he needed to take something for the pain, he wouldn't be laying here right now," she said sadly.

"Don't talk like that. You had no idea. The police will get to the bottom of it, I'm sure." He had his doubts about that but kept it to himself.

"Get some sleep. I'll just be in the other room if you need me. If he wakes up, yell," he nodded and left.

Abbi turned the lights out, all but one over the sink. She walked over to the fold-up bed, undid the strap, and pulled the legs down.

Ben groaned. It felt like a runaway moose had hit him. His body ached everywhere; in muscles he didn't even know he had. Try as he might, he couldn't open his eyes, they felt so heavy. A faint breeze caressed his brow, as he felt himself drifting back into the darkness. His last thought was of Abbi.

Abbi whipped her head around. *I did just hear him, right?* Dropping the legs with a bang, she rushed to his side, peering at his face. She took his hand in hers, praying he'd open his beautiful eyes. "Ben?" she whispered. She wanted so badly to crawl up beside him to hold him. *Dear God, if you're up there, please keep him safe...* She sat down on the chair, resting her arms on the edge of the bed.

She felt the tears sting her tired eyes while her gaze never wavered from his face. Burying her head in the crook of her arm, she cried herself to sleep.

Ben slowly came to. He felt Abbi's small hand in his.

He could feel her presence beside him but had no clue where he was. *Am I in my bed or hers and why is she down by my hip?* Was it that rough of a night that he couldn't remember? The last thing he did remember was looking up at her. Her telling him she loved him. He tried to gather the strength to squeeze her hand, to see if she was awake... His mouth felt like he had eaten a tablespoon of salt. He was so unbelievably thirsty. "Abbi?" he croaked. He moved his hand to her hair, catching a silky curl between his fingers, he gently tugged on the strand. "Abbi. Love. You awake?" He was so bloody tired and itchy. He brought his hand to scratch his face. *What the?...* He saw a needle taped down to the back of it. A tube running from it. He followed its path to a stand nearby. *Huh, an IV? How did that get there and why?...*

He had to do something, anything to quench his thirst. He immediately thought of his mum's pickled beets and felt the spring of saliva rush in his mouth. "Abbi!" he said, rubbing her hair.

Her head popped up; a bit of drool had dried to the corner of her mouth. "What....?" she looked at Ben through her hair. "Oh, thank you God!" she leaped up. Happy tears splashed from her eyes as she covered his face with kisses.

Catching her chin in his hand, his eyes pleaded with her. "Love, I need a drink, please."

"Yes, of course!" Rushing to the sink, she snatched a paper cup, filled it with water and returned to his side. "Here, let me help you," she said. Pulling the side tray close, she sat the water down, while she pulled on the mechanism to lift the head of the bed. "Good?" she asked.

At his nod, she grabbed the cup, bringing it to his lips. He drank it down in two gulps.

"Um... you should have probably just sipped that," she smiled.

"Couldn't help it, my mouth felt like a parched lake," he smiled at her. Ben looked around, not recognizing the room they were in. "Are we at the clinic?"

Abbi nodded. "Yes. Um... I'll go get Doc, give me a second."

"No, please tell me what happened. I can only remember you telling me you loved me." A look of confusion crossed his handsome face. "I can't remember anything after that."

"Do you remember taking that pain pill?"

"The one you broke in half. Yeah, I remember. You mean that pill put me here?" his brows shot up in question.

"Um." Her brow creased, casting sad eyes at him she said, ... "Yes. I'm so sorry Ben."

He reached out to her. Abbi backed away, catching the hurt in his eyes.

"I'm sorry. I did that to you," she hurried on so he couldn't interrupt. "You were sitting on the ground in front of me. You looked up at me asking what Kim and I had been laughing about." She started to pace as she recounted the events. "I told you nothing...that it was just girl talk." She paused, touching her lips at the memory of that last kiss they had shared before....

"I told you I loved you and you said... I love you... more," her voice broke on the last word.

"Right. It's true you know," he told her quietly.

She frowned at him. "So you say. Anyway, you looked so tired."

He watched the emotions play across her face.

A look of sorrow was there now, tugging at his heart.

"We were holding hands, and I noticed how cold yours felt," she explained.

He moved over in the bed. "Come here, love." he said, lifting the sheet.

She resisted the urge for a millisecond. She couldn't help it. Not needing to be asked twice, she quickly climbed up beside him. Laying her head on his shoulder as he tucked her to his side.

"Where was I?" she asked, looking up at him.

He squinted in thought. ".... Ah... I said I loved you more," he teased.

"No. That wasn't it.... Oh, that's right! Your hand was like ice," she nodded, staring at his Adam's apple. "The fireworks had started as we held hands. After five minutes or so, yours went limp." She looked up at him. "My first thought was that you had fallen asleep, but with all the noise I knew that wasn't possible." Tears started to well up in her eyes again as the scene replayed in her mind.

"Go on love, I'm here now," he murmured, brushing his lips across her forehead.

She closed her eyes. She took a steadying breath. "I called to you, but you didn't answer. I tried again and still no response." She touched his neck right where she had felt for his pulse earlier that night. "I put my hand, right here," she said laying hers against the steady, strong beat that was there now. She opened her eyes, tilting her head to gaze into his eyes. "I felt for your heartbeat. Oh, God, it was so slow," she sniffed, swallowing the tears that threatened.

Burying her face against his neck, she mumbled. "It felt like it was getting slower with every beat. I screamed for Kim to help you! She pushed me out of the way and started to work on you immediately." She looked up at him again. "She's a nurse, you know."

Placing his cheek on hers, he nodded. "Yes, I know, my sweet one," he murmured against her ear.

She laid her head on his shoulder. "Kim yelled to Ava to call Doc and told the guys to help her move you onto your back. She checked your pulse, your eyes and your mouth, and throat." She looked back up at him. "She smacked me across the face."

Ben chuckled. "She did, did she?" he asked, smiling. His love for her shining in his eyes.

"Yeah, she did." She wrapped her arms tight around him. "I froze. I didn't want to leave you. She told me to go ask your parents if you were allergic to anything."

He bit his lip shaking his head. "I'm not, at least nothing that I'm aware of."

"That's what they said. After running back, Doc showed up shortly thereafter. Kim told him what she thought was wrong; he examined you and came to the same conclusion...." she fell silent.

"Which was?" he asked, hedging for an answer.

She couldn't bring herself to say it, instead, she said, "Doc took a syringe, and stabbed it into a vial. He filled it and jammed it into your arm." She rubbed the spot where the needle had punctured his skin. "It was Naloxone." She looked up at him then. Laying her hand against his jaw, she quietly said, "It's what they give to reverse the effects of a drug overdose." She took a deep breath. "Doc didn't send those pills to the house, Ben. When you didn't pick up the first prescription, he didn't bother with another one.

Someone deliberately did this to you."

Tears streamed down her face. She had to tell him; she couldn't do this to him anymore. She couldn't allow anything to happen to him again.

She mourned for the loss that would come with it, but she had to let Ben go.

She lightly placed her lips on his, savoring their feel against her own. The taste of him, mingled with her tears ingraining it all for a memory. She'd forever love him. She loved him so much that she would let him go; she had to.

Ben felt a shift in Abbi's emotions. This wasn't just pain or guilt. This was something else she was feeling. Leaning back, Ben broke off the kiss to look her in the eyes. *What is she thinking about?* Noting the look of despair on her beautiful face, it hit him like a blow to the balls. "Abbi. I know what you're thinking of doing and you can forget about it," he said, giving her a dark look.

"No, you don't," she said, shocked when she saw that look in his eyes. *Damn it, he did!* "Ben, you can't stop me…"

He cut her off. "Like hell, I can't. Neither one of us is going anywhere… I've waited my whole life to find this kind of love and I'm not walking away from it, understood?" he said firmly.

Abbi was getting mad. "Fine… don't, then. But I can. I *need* to," she said getting off the bed.

"You would give up what we have over something like this?" he asked, scowling at her.

"You didn't see what happened to you. You could have *died*, Ben. And it would have all been because of me," she jabbed her chest. "Don't you see?" She touched his arm. "I can leave you because of how much I love you." She said with quiet determination, "It's the only way that *I* can protect you…" her voiced cracked.

"No! I don't see. And it's not happening. This was a fluke, okay?"

She snickered in disgust. "Ha! Oh no, it wasn't! This was not a fluke; someone has it out for you. That bottle had your name on it. If only I hadn't persisted that you take them." She rubbed her throbbing head.

Pulling out his IV, he shoved the covers back, swinging his legs over the edge he sat for a minute. He closed his eyes, his head swimming with dizziness. With the same determination as her, he slowly slid his feet to the floor.

"Just what do you think you're doing?" she hissed at him.

He ignored her of course. Pushing himself off the bed, he took the few steps to where she stood and took her in his arms. "We will get through this." He added gently, "… together."

She was like a lit firecracker ready to go off at any second. He felt relief when she relaxed within the circle of his arms.

Kissing her on the top of her head, he said, "I told you once I would go to the ends of the earth for you." He lifted her face to look into her eyes. "I meant it. If there's one thing in this world that is worth fighting for, it's love. You, my love, are worth it," he said, kissing her as if his very life depended on it.

She responded by wrapping her arms around his neck, smoothing the hair at the nape of his neck. Why couldn't she resist him? She was foolish to even think she could ever leave this man. To push him away was insane.

He pulled back, looking at her lips. He started chuckling.

"What's so funny?" she asked.

He touched the corner of her mouth. "You have a bit of something here," he said, rubbing the spot.

Good Lord! I drooled when I was sleeping, didn't I? Reaching up, she felt the area his fingers were currently trying to smooth away. "For cripes sake!" She dropped her arms and stalked to the sink. Turning the cold tap on, she splashed water on the spot and for good measure her whole face too. She grabbed some paper towel, patting her face dry, she looked to where he'd been standing. He was slowly making his way back to the bed.

Ben lifted the covers. "Come on love, let's get some sleep before we go home."

"I should let Doc know that you're awake."

"Leave him Abbi, let the man sleep. I'm fine, still a bit tired, a little itchy but otherwise I feel normal," he said, patting the bed.

She climbed up silently, snuggling up to his chest as he hugged her to him.

"Are you sure you're comfortable, I can sleep on the cot there," she said, motioning a hand towards the fold-up bed.

"Yeah, I'm fine. Get some rest. I love you, sweet one," he breathed with a contented sigh.

"And I love you… more."

She felt his chest shake with laughter, a satisfied smile on her lips as her eyes grew heavy. She realized he was right. Together they could get through this. Being apart would only be torture.

Chapter 9

"Hey guys, can everyone come and sit for a minute," Luke called from the dining table. "We have to hash out some details."

Once everyone was present, Lane cleared his voice to begin. "OK, so let's figure this out," he said, smacking a notebook on the table. Flicking a pen, he held his hand, poised to write. "Mom started getting phone calls, when?" He looked at Abby.

"Oh, hmm. Like I said before, at least six months; a year tops… maybe." She glanced at Ben, knowing it would upset him with her admission.

He sighed, shaking his head, a dark look on his face as he raised a brow at her. "Really?" He inclined his head towards her.

"Yeah," she nodded. "But in my defense, they were always unknown numbers."

Ben pursed his lips and nodded his head. "Right. Can I see your phone Abbi?" he asked, holding out his hand.

"Of course." She passed it to him. She watched him take the case and remove the back. Next, he took out the battery. Taking the card out, he bent it in half. She grabbed his arm. "What did you do *that* for!" she cried in alarm, stunned that he had the audacity to do that.

"Good thinking, Ben. Mom, you will need to get a new card, your phone is useless for the time being," Luke said, looking at her.

Abbi stared at Luke like he was an idiot for siding with Ben.

Ben took her hand, leaned towards her, and held the bent card in his fingers. "I did that because this can trace you."

"Oh," she said flatly.

"Yeah," he mumbled, dropping the card.

"OK, what else do we know?" Lane persisted.

"Shortly after I moved in, you heard music and laughing you said, right?" Ben looked to her for confirmation.

"Yes. That was before we met. I didn't know you had moved in yet. I thought your house was still empty." She looked at everyone gathered around the table. Feeling the need to explain. "I tripped over the bottom step and landed flat on my face," she told them.

"How long has that step been waiting to get fixed?" Ava asked snickering.

"Since the day you moved in at least." Kim laughed. "Looks good on you," she smiled sweetly.

"Yes. Well, someday I'll get around to it."

A yelp from the backyard had everyone turning their head… all except Abbi, who froze. She heard that cry of pain before. Slowly getting up, she went to the back door. Lucy was lying on the porch, Brutus and Molly were playing in the yard. A little too rough she supposed. The dogs were otherwise fine. But that cry of pain….

Walking back to the table, she thought back to that day she met Ben at Mack's. She had been so pissed off when she found out he had bought the place, that she had called Nigel. When she'd gotten home, the animals were all waiting for her at the window, Brutus howling his head off. She remembered she had gone outside with them, sitting down in a chair on the porch. That's when she heard the same yelping cry that Molly had just done. *Oh my God!*

No wonder Brutus was so protective of Molly. It was her cries they'd heard. She came back into the dining area where everyone else was.

She grabbed the back of Ben's chair; she felt like she was about to hurl.

Racing to the bathroom, she made it to the tub, retching her guts out.

"Abbi?" Ben was at her side, rubbing her back. "Are you okay, love?" he asked. He pulled her hair back as she threw up a second time. He got up and wet a washcloth. "Here, sweet one," he crooned to her as if she were a baby.

Taking it from him, she mopped her face as she sat on the floor, her back against the tub.

"You okay now?" he asked, as he went down on his knees before her. She nodded shakily. "What was that all about?" he motioned to the tub. A movement caught his eye. Raising his brows in disbelief. He saw Void, her stubby-legged cat, sitting in the tub at the far end patiently waiting for her to finish so he could get a drink. He gave Ben an expectant meow.

Grabbing the cat, Ben set him on the floor, giving him a gentle push towards the door. He turned back, and took the handheld shower head and rinsed the tub. Going to the vanity, he opened the door under the sink and grabbed the cleaner and a sponge. He knelt before Abbi. Taking a hold of her waist, he slid her over and out of the way. He methodically scrubbed, waiting for her to answer.

"Love?" he hedged.

"Yeah?" She looked at him blankly.

"You want to tell me something?"

"Yeah, Um. That night when we first met, before you came over with the flowers… I heard a dog screaming in pain from across the lake… like directly across." She grabbed his arm.

"Ben. You were right all along. I think it was Molly..." She trailed off imagining the horrors that poor dog must have endured at the hands of pure evil. "And that's not all. There was a flash of light, too. I thought it was just headlights, but now I'm not so sure," she chewed her lip with worry.

He stopped and looked at her. "Huh...," was all he said, a thoughtful look on his face.

"What is it?"

He licked his lips, frowning as he bent to rinse the tub. "The other night. When you went into the house to get the painkillers, I saw a light too, directly across from the house. More of a reflection, really," he said absently.

"That's it! That's what I saw! Oh my God, how long have they been watching me?" She felt the sickness rise in her throat again. Shoving Ben aside she let it hurl again.

He pursed his lips. "Right!" he said, tossing the sponge down to rub her back again.

Kim looked up as Abbi and Ben walked back into the kitchen. "You look like shit!" she stated the obvious.

"Uh-huh, thanks, sis." Abbi rolled her eyes, sitting with a thud on the chair.

"So," Ben looked to the dogs that were now laying on the floor. "What we just discovered is that Molly here..." he motioned for her to come to him. "... was abused by whoever is doing this. Before it was just me speculating. But now Abbi is sure of it."

"What makes you think so Abbi?" Greg asked.

"When I heard her yelping a bit ago. I heard it the night Ben, and I met, just before he came over. There was what I thought a light across the lake and Ben said he saw one the other night, too." she said, hunkering down into her sweater.

"It's more of a reflection. Like light hitting off a lens," Ben supplied.

"Or maybe binoculars?" Mark asked.

"Yeah." Ben nodded in agreement. "Could have been that too."

"Well, there must have been more that's happened," Lane said. "This just can't be it," he frowned, waving a hand at the notebook.

Everyone sat quietly, trying to think if they remembered anything out of the ordinary in the last year.

"Well, there's the flowers and note," Kim said, looking at the table with a fixed stare.

"True, that is true," Nancy agreed.

Ben leaned an arm on the back of his chair, clasping his hands together. Abbi glanced at him. *He looks so relaxed how the hell does he do it?*

"Say. Did you find out anything more about Jacob Randal?" Ben asked Mark.

"Actually, my brother is doing a more in-depth search of the Ottawa area… calling the locals there. I thought he'd have gotten back to me by now but hasn't. I should call him maybe," Mark responded, sitting there.

Kim looked at him. "Uh. Yes, you should. What are you waiting for?"

"Of course! I'll just go do that now." Mark got up, taking his cell from his pocket. Dialing his brother's number, he walked outside onto the front porch.

"I'll be right back," Ava excused herself, walking out to the porch to join Mark.

"Could there be anything on that note that might give us a clue?" Luke asked. "Where did it go, where did the flowers go?"

"Now that I think about it. Those flowers looked like they had blood on them," Kim said. "And what about the prescription Ben got? That had the drugstore stickers on it," she suggested.

Shaking her head Abbi looked at her. "Doc told us before we left the clinic yesterday that he checked with the drugstore. A new employee had tossed some old labels in the garbage instead of shredding them. Whoever did it must have searched through the garbage and found them. It would be easy enough to print the directions on it." She sighed, bouncing her leg up and down. This was all becoming too much for her to handle.

Ben cleared his throat and laid a hand on Abbi's knee. "I threw the flowers along with the note in the weeds across the road," he said, rubbing his hand back and forth across her thigh. "They might offer a clue. But even so, they need to be tested at a lab and that would take weeks if not months."

Mark and Ava breezed back into the house. "Okay, guys… Steve looked into it further and it looks like there is no way that it's Jacob Randal"

Ben frowned. "How can he be so sure?" He was positive that it was him.

Sighing heavily, Mark said, "Because he's been in jail for 2 weeks. Sorry guys," he said, sitting down.

"Mom, have there been any strange cars around lately, anyone walking around?" Ava asked.

Abbi thought back. There was that car a few weeks ago… parked beside the lake. And the boat, not that either was out of the ordinary, but both had been close.

"Abbi. When was your break-in?" Ben asked quietly. He had a theory, but he just wanted to be certain before he mentioned it to everyone.

"The end of February, the twenty-seventh to be exact. I had been gone for a week. I had to meet with the director for the movie to go over some key points."

Ben looked at her in surprise. She read his mind.

"He couldn't come here. I had no choice but to meet him in Toronto," she explained.

He smiled, taking her hand, silently conveying his understanding.

His brow furrowed, Mark spoke up, "That's around the time shooting for the movie started. Abbi, do you have any enemies?" he queried.

Ben looked at Mark, at the mention of enemies, he had a flashback. That was something he'd need to investigate in his own past. No doubt he had a few.

"Ha, ha, ha." Kim burst out laughing. "Abbi have any enemies? That's a hoot! Maybe Sally Schmit from 5th grade! Didn't you put glue in her hair when she pissed you off for stealing your boyfriend?" She smacked the table, her laughter trailing off to giggly sighs.

Abbi smiled at the memory and nodded. "Yeah, I did. And then I braided it!" She laughed.

Ben grinned, leaning back. "How does that not surprise me?" he asked, folding his arms across his chest.

"She deserved it, we had only been dating for a week," she giggled.

"You were such a rebel mom," Ava laughed.

"Yeah, well. That's all behind me now," she smiled. *Not really. If Sally Schmit tried that today she'd be bald*, she thought wryly, as she glanced at Ben.

"Back on track here. So, no unusual cars or people around," Lane started to write on the paper.

"What about the boat?" Luke said.

Lane glanced up at him. "Boat?" he asked.

Luke shot a hand towards the lake. "Ben and Mom said there had been a boat out there. Right?" He looked to both Abbi and Ben for confirmation.

"Yeah," Ben replied, as Abbi nodded.

"Don't forget the boat we saw," Ava added, looking at Mark.

"Right, you said it was a rental?" Lane asked, writing it down. "What was the name again?" He looked up expectantly.

Ava rubbed her forehead in thought. "Pearl Lake Yacht and Boat rentals," she said, snapping her fingers.

"Good, so we have a lead, one of us needs to go over there and see if we can find out the name it was rented under," Greg said.

"I'll go." Ben volunteered.

Shaking her head Abbi was about to tell him no, when Kim said, "Nope, you can't."

He looked at her with a raise of his brows.

"Whoever did this, thinks you're dead, remember?"

"I'll wear a disguise," he said, blinking at her.

Shaking her head. "Sorry stud. But no disguise will hide that face." Kim pointed at her own, drawing an imaginary circle over it. "You need to stay on the down-low." She pushed her hand down to emphasize. "Like way down... low."

Noticing the look of panic on Abbi's face, Mark chimed in. "She's right, Ben. You need to stay here. Ava and I can go," he said, looking at her for encouragement.

Ava nodded. "Yeah, we were talking about checking it out when we saw it. A perfect reason to now."

"I can't expect any of you to stick around," Abbi said, looking at all of them, casting her gaze on each of her kids.

"You have lives to get back to in Windsor," she paused. "Traffic will be insane. No, you guys need to go," she added firmly.

"Mom, I've already told the girls I'm staying here for a bit," Ava said, coming over to hug her. "They will cover the spa for me."

Lane reached across the table to take hold of her hand. "I have to get back. I've got meetings all week Mom. Otherwise, you know I would stay," he said, squeezing her hand.

"We had a train package booked." Greg looked at Nancy. At her nod, he said, "But we will cancel and stick around."

"No, you can't do that!" Abbi cried out, tears springing to her eyes. She got up and went to them "It's your first time in Canada. You don't want to be stuck at my house." She bent, giving them each a hug. "Seriously you two, go have fun, I insist." She knew they had booked economy; she made a mental note to contact the train depot to change their tickets to first class, with the glass top roof. It was the least she could do for them.

Luke came over to Abbi. "I have to fly out of Toronto in the morning." He hugged her.

"Where are you headed this time?" she asked, holding onto her oldest for dear life.

"Not far… just to New York for a few days." He hugged her tight. "As much as I hate to, we will have to leave in about an hour or so, if I'm going to make it to Toronto before dark." He looked at Lane. "Will you be ready by then?"

"Yeah, just let me finish this up and I'll be ready."

"Aunt Kim, what are you doing?" Ava asked. "Can you stay, or do you have to leave too?"

"Sure, I'll stay. I've got a month off so I'm good… unless you guys want me to skedaddle," she said, looking to Abbi and Ben.

Ben looked Kim straight in the eyes. "I could never say no to the woman who saved my life," he murmured.

Kim blinked rapidly. "Oh! Myyy… God."

Abbi knew exactly what Kim was feeling at that very moment. When he used that tone of voice with her, he had her melting, every damn time.

Kim started waving her hand in front of her face. "Wow!" she was visibly flushed. Giggling, she glanced at Ben. "Do you have a brother somewhere?" She quickly turned to his parents. "Is he your only son?" she asked, her hand waving faster.

Nancy and Greg laughed at her. "Afraid so," Nancy said, nodding her head.

Jerking her head back around. A sneer on her lips, Kim rolled her eyes and mumbled, "Figures." She threw her head back and let out a cackle, laughing her fool head off causing everyone to join in.

Abbi stood watching Ben exchange goodbyes with his parents. Their car was packed and ready for the trip to Springbank. There, they would catch the train where their adventures would begin. Abbi had already changed the booking, so they were in for a surprise when they arrived. It was the least she could do to pay them back for bringing such a beautiful human into the world. Her boys had already left an hour ago amid a teary goodbye. Oh, how she'd miss them. She wanted them all to move up here with her when she made the move, but they had their own lives. She understood, but she so wished they would change their minds. Someday maybe…

Greg and Nancy were now backing out. Ben waved as he walked back towards the house. Careful to stay next to the house where no prying eyes could see him.

Moonlit Stalker

"Hey." She reached out a hand to him, smiling

"Hey yourself gorgeous," he growled, smiling at her.

"Now what do we do?" she sighed.

Even though they weren't alone, the house felt empty somehow.

"Oh, I have a few things in mind," he said, nuzzling her neck, drawing her tight against him.

"Mhm. I bet you do," she said, holding his head as he raked his lips across her skin to her throat.

The door opened just then. "Hey, oh man! Can't you guys keep your hands to yourselves for one minute?" Mark asked. "Like come on! Feel for the single people around here would ya?"

Ben laughed. "Sure buddy. What did you want?" he said, turning Abbi around and steering her into the house.

"Well. We decided…" Mark motioned towards Kim and Ava.

"That it would be best for you to stay in the house." He pointed at the floor with both hands. "This house… unless of course Abbi objects. If that's the case, then we need to move you in the dark to your house."

"That's absurd," Abbi snickered. "Why would I object?"

"Indeed," Kim looked at Ben and smiled. She flashed her eyes to Abbi, now a full grin on her face, giving her a wink along with a thumbs up.

Abbi just laughed shaking her head. "You're incorrigible, you know that, right?" Abbi asked her.

"I try." Kim laughed at herself.

Mark nodded. "Good, it's settled then. Us three will stay at Ben's."

"Abbi, you need to lie low too. The less you're seen outside, the more likely it will draw the perp out," Kim said.

"Nice cop lingo, Kim," Abbi nodded.

"I know, right!" Kim laughed.

"Come on, Aunt Kim. It's time we got out of their hair," Ava said.

They all scattered in different directions gathering up their belongings to take over to Ben's house.

Ben came to her, taking her in his arms, he jerked her to him. "Love. What shenanigans can we get into, I wonder?" he murmured.

She looked at him. He took her breath away. A hunger she had never seen before in his eyes burned over her skin. She smoothed her hands down his chest. "I have a trick or two up my sleeve," she smiled sweetly.

Just you wait and see...

Chapter 10

"You know I could get used to living here," Kim said as the three of them made their way on the path to Ben's house.

"Yeah?" Mark asked. "I know what you mean. Here I had this place for three years and only came to it once or twice," he said, waving his hand at the house.

"What! Are you crazy?" Kim looked in awe at Ben's house. Abbi's place was a dump compared to this. She especially loved the fact that the lake was all around it, except for the adjoining land between the two properties. Otherwise it was as if it was an island.

"I bet you're kicking yourself now?" Ava chimed in, looking around too.

"Careful, watch the branch," Mark said, holding it so it didn't swat one of them in the face. "Well, after Ben moved in, I came up... a few weeks ago now and yeah, I was kicking myself. But I have since figured out that if I stayed, I wouldn't have met you, fine ladies, now would I?" he said, raising his brows.

"True, that is very true," Kim said. "Or we would have met under different circumstances and we might have hated you," she laughed.

"Don't laugh, I hated myself too," he said, climbing the steps. Maybe it was age, but ever since meeting Abbi and her family, Mark felt like his wild ways were a thing of the past. Mark stopped, shocked at the revelation. *Whoa! Man, where did that come from?* Glancing at Ava he realized he knew exactly where that came from.... the Peterson women were witches.

"Shit, what the hell is that?" Ava asked, looking at the step.

Peering down Kim said, "Huh... that must be the blood Ben was talking about."

Not moving, she followed the trail with her eyes, to where it had stopped at the door and pooled there. "Oh, hell no!" She looked up at the others. "We need to catch this bastard now."

"Sooner, rather than later," Mark nodded.

Ava just stood frozen to the spot. "If someone can hurt Molly like that... Just what will they do to Mom or Ben, given the chance?" she asked with worry.

"Hey, it's okay." Mark draped an arm around Ava's shoulders. "There's five of us and only one of them... well, maybe. We don't have a clue how many we are dealing with."

Ava's face took on a horrified look at the possibility that there could be more than one person.

"Nice going, Sherlock! Now you've scared the crap out of her," Kim stated the obvious as she reached out to comfort Ava.

"I'm sorry. But the reality is..."

Kim pointed a finger under his nose, effectively cutting him off. Shaking her head, she said, "Nope, no. You will not finish that thought. Would you just open the damn door already?" She had to restrain her foot from kicking him in the ass.

Opening cans of cat and dog food had the brood running to the kitchen. Bird came soaring in, squawking his delight. Poor guy had to be caged for the last few days while everyone was there.

"Ben, are you hungry?" Abbi asked, dumping the food into the dishes. She glanced towards him as she set them on the floor.

He was sitting at the table, her laptop in front of him. He was staring intently at the screen, running his finger across his bottom lip.

She went to the cupboard, got a scoop of Bird's peanuts, and walked into the library.

Dumping the peanuts into the cage, Abbi checked to make sure there was enough water. "Hey Birdie, come and get it."

Ben was doing some checking of his own. He couldn't stop thinking about Mark asking if Abbi had any enemies. He had doubted very much that she did. But he wouldn't rule out himself for not having any.

"Hey, love! Can you come here a minute, please?"

Turning on her heel, she went to see what he wanted.

He pulled her to his side. "Here, look. Have you seen this guy around here at all?" he asked, pointing at the screen.

She bent closer to get a good look. Ben took a hold of her hips pulling her down so she could sit on his legs.

Frowning, she thought he looked a bit familiar but couldn't place him. Abbi shook her head. "Hmm, not that I can remember." She looked at him. "Why?" she asked.

"You're sure?" He bit his bottom lip. "Look again… please."

She thought for a minute. "Am I supposed to know him?" she asked, looking intently at the screen.

"Does he or doesn't he look like the guy that bumped into you outside of the mall in Springbank?" he pointed to his face.

"Well, the guy had a winter hat and gloves on," she looked at him. "I found that a bit odd for this time of year." She looked back at the screen.

"His face Abbi… look at his face," he urged patiently.

She turned her head to the side. "Now that you mention his face… yeah! It looks like him." She felt him immediately tense under her. "Why….?"

***

"Mark, can you slow down a bit?" Kim called from the back seat of Ben's car.

Kim wasn't used to riding in the back seat, especially in a little black sports car with only two doors and a hatch that she could never in her wildest dreams smash her fat ass through, if the need arose.

"I'm only going ten kilometers an hour! How slow do you want me to go, woman?" Mark asked incredulously.

She was squished in a corner with clothes spread out beside her. The road was so bendy she didn't want them scuttling on her. "Five kilometers is good." She wrinkled her nose as she picked up a black article of clothing. *Is this stuff even clean?* She held it up between two fingers. She turned it this way and that. Realizing it was a pair of men's boxer briefs… Ben's boxer briefs, she whipped them to the floor. "Hey, can you open a window, it's getting a little…stuffy in here," she gulped, pulling her collar away to get some airflow going.

Mark glanced at Ava. "Is she always like this?" he raised his brows, his eyes large in his face.

"She's worse when she gets to know you better," Ava grinned out the passenger window.

Mark gave her a double take. "You're kidding, right?"

"Stop talking about me. I can hear you know," Kim said, getting hotter by the minute. "Ava crack your damn window! Now, before I barf on these clothes here," she motioned with her hand.

That's all it took. Both front windows were down in seconds, as the car crept painfully slow toward the boat rentals.

***

"I'm just not quite ready to share what I'm thinking at the moment," Ben said looking into her eyes. "I need to be 100% sure before I say anything."

"Not even a hint?" Abbi smiled.

"No love, not even a hint," he said, dropping a kiss on her nose. He closed the laptop with a snap. "What shall we eat?" he asked.

"Funny you should ask," she said, getting up. "The food here is just about depleted. I could order a pizza or have Mack drop off something?" she suggested.

"Would he do that?"

"Yeah. He does it all the time, especially when I'm in writer's mode," she said, walking to the fridge to see exactly what they would need.

"I'll just get him to cook us up something for tonight and bring a few groceries for the next few days," she said. "What do you feel like eating?"

He raised a brow. "Tonight? You for starters," he murmured. A thrill of delight skimmed up her spine at his words.

"Uh…well, we'll see about that." She felt the heat rise to her cheeks.

He grinned. "How about burgers and fries? I could go for that. My first meal here was one of Mack's burgers."

"They're amazing, aren't they," she agreed, nodding her head. Picking up the cordless house phone she dialed Mack's number. Rummaging through the freezer, she waited for him to pick up.

"Don't tell him I'm here," Ben said in a loud whisper.

She gave him a quick nod and sent a dazzling smile his way.

"Hey, Mack… I'm good! How are you?" Her smile turned into a laugh. "Yeah, that is so true. But what can we expect, right? It's tourist season!" She paused, listening. "Really?"

Ben thought she sounded surprised; her expression confirmed it as he watched her features change from amusement to a frown, all while she kept the happy, upbeat tone with Mack going.

"Right?!" she nodded. "Yeah, I was calling to see if I could order some burgers and fries, and a few items to last me the week here."

"Ah yes, two burgers and two orders of fries. Actually, can you make the fries into poutine?" She smiled as Ben gave her a thumbs up. "No. I uh, plan on just eating the other one tomorrow, you know how I am when I'm writing... No, Ben's not here. His parents were down... yes... um, yeah. He went back to England with them. He's just gone... I guess." She rubbed her forehead; she did that a lot lately.

Ben could tell she hated lying to Mack. He went over to her and rubbed the tension from her neck and shoulders. She sighed softly at his touch as she placed the grocery order.

"Great thanks, Mack, see you soon." She ended the call. "God, I hate lying to that man." Turning around she put her hand on her hip, a thoughtful look on her face.

"What is it?" Ben asked.

"Mack just said that business is picking up." How was she going to tell him what Mack had just said? *If I do, he will charge out of the house the second it passes my lips...*

He looked at her, his brows raised in question. "And...? Is that unusual or something?"

"Um...No... not at all." No, she'd keep it to herself. For now, there was no cause to tell him about the man currently sitting at Mack's, eating a fried Bologna sandwich. A man, Mack referred to as a real loony... considering it was a warm sunny day, too warm to be wearing a winter hat and gloves.

She pasted a smile on her lips. "Mack said he will be here in about an hour. He's just waiting on a customer to leave."

Ben nodded. "Sounds good. I'll just do a little more research, if you don't mind?" he said, looking at the laptop.

"No, go ahead. I'm going to head out to the garage for a minute."

Lifting the lid of the laptop, he waved a hand, already engrossed in the screen before him. "I'll be here," he said absently.

Abbi crossed the room to the short hall that led to the attached garage. She never used it, only for storage. Glancing around, she heaved a heavy sigh. There were boxes upon boxes piled high against the wall, along with furniture from the previous owner. Maybe she'd have a yard sale, once everything was back to normal. That was if she could get everything in order first. She grabbed the closest box. Rifling through it, she saw the kids' Mother's Day cards and gifts made from their school days, falling apart and faded with age. They would think she was nuts for keeping all of it. It certainly wouldn't be the first time, she chuckled as she closed the box and put it in the keep pile.

Moving a rug that had been tossed and forgotten, she found an old cd player beneath it. It wasn't hers. She frowned looking at it, as she sat it on a table. Plugging it in she hit the power button. It turned on. Now to find something to play on it. Moving another box aside, she located CDs in an old milk crate. Sitting on the concrete floor, she flipped through them. She was an 80's music kinda gal. This stuff was all… classical? She found one that she thought might do. Getting up she popped the CD out of the case as she walked to the player. Pushing the open button, she softly blew in it removing the dust. Closing the door, she waited for the music to start. A thundering of beating drums followed by the soothing sounds of a cello set the mood for her cleaning.

Abbi got to work clearing most of the floor up, there were still a few boxes left to break down and one more to add to the others, but that was the end of the clutter scattered about. She glanced at her watch. *Mack should be here shortly*, she thought, grabbing the last box.

Casting an eye around the room to see where the best place to stick it would be, she decided next to a mirror that was hanging on the wall. She looked down at her clothes, wondering if she'd have time to hop in for a quick shower real. No. She couldn't miss Mack and she certainly couldn't let Ben open the door when he was supposed to be on the other side of the world. She frowned, staring out the window. She hated lying to Mack but what choice did she have; he was a talker… not an intentional gossiper, but he did let things slip.

Where in the world was that music coming from, Ben wondered. Was that the same music Abbi previously heard? He got up from the table to find the source. He hoped not, as it was coming from the garage. *Where did Abbi say she was going?* He had been so engrossed with searching the web that he hadn't heard her leave. He followed the sounds of the music and stopped. She was standing by the window looking out, her arms folded across her chest. And she took his breath away. Her clothes were dusty, her hair a mess with what looked like a cobweb in it. Yet, she was still the most beautiful woman he had laid eyes on. He glanced over and saw the source of the music. He moved to it and saw the milk crate full of CD's. Selecting one, he hit the open/close button on the player and swapped the disks.

Abbi turned when the music cut out. She watched Ben as he changed the disks. She held out her hand to him as he crossed the floor to her.
Ben took it while the sounds of a piano filled the garage. His other hand snaked around her waist, pulling her to him.

"Dance with me, my love." He touched his lips to her temple as he brought their hands to his chest.

"This song describes what I feel for you, perfectly," he murmured, gazing into her eyes, a soft smile on his lips.

John Legend's voice crooned out the song 'All of Me', as they swayed back and forth.

Listening to the words, Abbi's eyes filled with tears. She wrapped her arms around his neck so tight, never wanting to let go.

"It's true, Abbi," he murmured, rubbing her back.

She leaned back, looking into his eyes. She kissed him softly. Knowing she didn't deserve someone as beautiful as him. She ran her thumb across his bottom lip. "I love you so much and I will no matter what happens. Okay?" she asked as a single tear left a wet trail down her dusty cheek.

"Abbi, I feel the same way. Nothing will happen or ever change that," he said adamantly. "Now please, stop thinking it will. Because baby, you're stuck with me." He smiled nuzzling her neck, that caused an eruption of giggles to pass over her lips as the song slowly ended.

"Abbi, are you in there?" They heard Mack knocking on the garage door.

"Shit, duck down," she whispered. "It's Mack, and you're in England, remember?"

Ducking down, Ben looked around. *Just how is he going to see me? ...* There were no windows in any of the doors.

"Coming, Mack... I'll meet you at the front door," she yelled, hurrying off into the house to greet him at the door.

Ben stayed put. Waiting for the all-clear from Abbi, he stood looking around, and saw she had a lot of boxes to go through yet. He flipped open the flaps of one nearest to him. *Huh, a box full of yearbooks, cool...*

Taking one he glanced at the year... 1984. He put it back, looking to see if there were any from Abbi's high school days. He pulled one out from 1989.

That was the year before the boys were born, she was only 15. God, at 15 he was into cars and drama class. He couldn't imagine having to raise a baby at that age, let alone twins.

He flipped it open, scanning the names listed alphabetically. Running his finger down, he realized he didn't know if Peterson was her married name or her maiden name... maiden. There she was Abbi Peterson.

A young girl stared up at him from the page, a soft smile on her lips. She was older now, wiser and more beautiful. He couldn't help but feel protective of the girl back then. He scanned the page, wondering if she had met her husband in school too. He could hear her coming through the short hall to the garage. *Mack must have left,* he thought. He was just about to snap it closed, when a familiar face caught his eye. *What the hell?* ...

Frowning. he looked at the name. There was no way that could be his name. He peered closer. But it was him! All this time he had been searching on the web for any background info and here it was in Abbi's garage the whole time. In the black-and-white photo, there was a younger version of the man Ben knew, but not the name he had now. The very man that wanted the lead for Abbi's book. They never gave him a chance to audition. Tony, the director knew exactly who he'd cast if they wanted the part.

Ben couldn't refuse it.

Chapter 11

"What do you *mean* you can't tell us who rented a boat a few days ago?" Kim snapped at the attendant.

"Ma'am, it's against company policy to divulge the names of our customers to other people."

Mark grabbed Kim by the arms, dragging her out of the way. Giving the attendant his most charming smile, he said, "Look...," dropping his eyes to the name tag, "Deloris. She meant nothing by that," he said, trying to calm the situation. "What she meant was, how much would it be to rent a boat for say... ten minutes?" he inquired, pulling his wallet out of his back pocket.

Deloris rolled her eyes, "We don't do ten-minute rentals. If you want to step foot on a boat, it's a minimum hourly rental, which is $100.00 plus tax." She replied snootily, giving them a look as if they couldn't afford it.

Kim gasped in shock.

"We'll take it." Ava smacked two $100 dollar bills on the counter. "But we want that one," she said, pointing out the window to the largest boat sitting at the dock.

Deloris changed her attitude quickly at the sight of the bills, "Certainly. I just need you to sign right here." She passed a clipboard over to Ava who signed with a flourish.

"Come on," Ava said to the others, leading the way to the door.

Pointing at Deloris, Kim couldn't help but get the last word in.

She raised her brows. "Just an FYI. That's robbery!" she exclaimed, scurrying out the door after Ava and Mark.

Mark was busy steering the boat towards Abbi's house. He wanted to know how easy it would be to see into her house from a hundred feet out.

"So… what exactly are we looking for again?" Kim asked for the tenth time.

"Anything," Ava answered. She bent down, wrinkling her brow in disgust at a squashed dead bug. "Anything that could be a clue."

"Well, it's kind of pointless, isn't it? I mean, they would clean the boats between customers, you would think." Kim mumbled, searching the floor for anything that didn't fit.

Ava went down in the cabin below. Opening doors and drawers as she went. *There has got to be something here...*

There was. A horrid smell. She couldn't quite discern where it was coming from. Glancing around, Ava spied a wastebasket under the sink. She pulled it out, peering into it, and jerked her head back and immediately gagged. She had to get to fresh air. Now! Blindly turning on her heel, she stumbled up the steps taking two at a time. "Look," she said shoving the basket under Kim's nose, as she dry heaved, "What is it?"

Kim backed away. "Ava, what the hell?" She wrinkled her nose in disgust. "What is that God awful smell?"

Carefully setting it down, Ava too backed away. "I don't know. It smells dead, whatever it is."

Mark glanced over his shoulder, the smell wafting to him now. "That smells like shit. Ava, dump it out," he said.

Ava's eyes snapped to his face. "Here?" she exclaimed, disgusted at the thought. "Like… on the floor?"

He shrugged. "Yeah sure… why not?"

Ava looked at the basket with revulsion as if it were a snake. Balancing on one foot, she tipped it over with her boot, standing it upside down. Then for no reason at all, she kicked it like it was a soccer ball. Her screams of disgust shattering the stillness of the lake. The trees came alive as birds took flight in every direction.

"Holy Montana!" Mark ducked as it sailed over his head, landing with a plop in the water.

"What the hell is wrong with you…screaming like that? I almost pissed my pants!" Kim hissed.

"I'm sorry! It's just so disgusting…" Ava bent over peering at the contents. "Oh… It's just rotten hamburger." She snatched a crumpled piece of paper stuck to the dried blood on the cellophane, scrutinizing it.

They were about 100 yards out from Abbi's shoreline Mark judged. Just what he thought… a perfect view. He could see everything in the yard and on the porch. But not in the house; that would likely change at nightfall. Killing the engine, he walked to Ava, looking over her shoulder. "What is it?" He squinted trying to figure out what was written on the paper.

"I don't know." She frowned. "It looks like it's written in blood. Uh, didn't Ben say the note mom got, looked like it was too?" she scowled, looking at Mark.

"Let me see that." Kim snatched it away. Shaking her head, she tsked, "Whoever wrote this has terrible penmanship. It says… I'm coming…." She brought it closer to her eyes, "… for you. Raven Black." Looking up, her face screwed with confusion. "Who is Raven Black? How many people is this person after?"

Mark stood there shaking his head. Disbelief on his face. "I know that guy," he pointed at the note.

"You do?" Ava felt a rush of relief, finally, a lead.

He gave a quick nod of his head. "Yeah. He wanted Ben's part in the Jasper Killings."

"We need to tell them. Can you get closer to the shore?"

"Yeah, sure. Ben has a dock over at his place." Mark started the engine, in less than a minute, they were pulling up to the dock.

"We can't stay long. This thing has to be back soon," Mark said, wrapping the line around a post. "Come on."

All three of them ran along the shore to Abbi's yard. The sun casting long shadows as they made their way to the back porch.

Just as Ava raised her fist to pound on the French doors, Mark grabbed her arm.

"Wait! Don't do that!" he whispered loudly.

"Do what?"

"Shh, keep your voice down!" he hushed her.

"Why?" Ava shook her head, her eyes growing large. *"What the hell is your problem?" she asked, raising her voice.*

"They might be, you know… busy." He gave her a look.

"Busy at what?"

Rolling her eyes, Kim piped up. "Sex, Ava. They might be getting it on, is what he's trying to say." She reached around Ava and pounded on the glass herself.

"Tell me… is everyone in your family so inconsiderate?" Mark asked, folding his arms across his chest with a huff.

"Only when assholes are threatening us," Kim grinned.

"Hey handsome, the coast is clear. Mack just left," Abbi said, peeking into the garage.

"Abbi, look." Ben came to her with one of her old high school yearbooks, pointing at a photo. "Look who it is."

She took it in her hands, glancing to where he had pointed. She looked at him. "Yeah, that's Roland Eddy. What about him?"

She walked into the kitchen. Ben followed, going to the table.

"It's him," he said, grabbing the laptop to show her.

"No, that's... Raven Black," she looked up from the screen.

"It's the same guy, Abbi," he groaned in frustration. "Look, I'll show you." He sat the laptop on the table. Using his hands, he covered everything in the photo except the man's face.

Abbi sat down, holding the yearbook beside the screen for comparison. She laid the book down and walked to the counter to get their food. "Okay, I see it now. So, what does this mean?" She looked at him as she grabbed the forks. "Well?" She asked, after he didn't respond. Opening the fridge she took a bottle of ketchup and grabbed two cans of pop. He watched her as she walked towards him with her hands full. "Well, I had a theory, but I'm not so sure now." He sighed, taking his food from her.

"Which is?" She sat down and opened hers. Taking a bite of her burger, she looked at him.

Holding up a finger, Ben took a mouthful of poutine and groaned in delight. He pointed to his food. "This is better than that place in the mall."

"Mack is a man of many talents that's for sure," she smiled. "Now quit stalling Ben and tell me, what's your theory?"

"Well. When Mark asked if you had any enemies... it got me wondering if I did." He chewed thoughtfully. "Mack needs to branch out, has he thought of franchising?"

"Already asked him. I even told him I would back him, but he isn't interested."

Nodding, he said, "Right, fair enough."

She looked at him through her lashes. "Do you have any enemies, Ben?" She couldn't imagine why he would.

"Um... Yeah, most likely." He didn't want to come right out and say yes... because of the film. No doubt, she'd blame herself for that.

"Roland Eddy?" she hedged. She needed to know. Roland had

always had a crush on her. Throughout school, he'd asked her out on a date. She kindly declined, but that never stopped him from asking. After she found out she was pregnant, she left school, never going back. She had no idea what happened to him.

Ben licked his lips, leaning back in his chair. Abbi could see that he was stalling.

"Ben just tell me. We are in this together, remember?" she repeated the words he had told her so many times.

Pushing his food away, he sighed heavily, choosing his words carefully for her sake.

"Well, I can't be certain." He reached to take her hand. "But Raven Black wanted the part that I got…"

The dogs raced through the house to the French doors in the living room, growling and barking as they passed by.

"Who the hell is that?" he said, shooting out of his chair to see.

"Ben! Get back. We don't know who it is." Abbi rushed to get up to see who was pounding on her door. Relief flowed over her.

"It's okay, it's Kim and them." She unlocked the door, swinging it wide. "Hey guys, come on in."

"Hey, Abbi. Ben around here?" Mark asked, searching the room.

She could see the concern etched on his face.

Coming around the corner Ben said, "Yeah, right here mate. What's up?"

"Good… we need to talk." He looked pointedly at Abbi.

"It's fine. Abbi and I were just talking about what's going on." Ben looked at her. Softly he said, "We're in this together."

"Good, because we found something." Kim rushed on.

"So did we." Ben motioned for them to follow him into the kitchen.

"Us first," Kim said, interrupting Ben before he could say a thing.

"Alright, what do you have?"

"Well, first off. Dude, you need to clean your car out." She wrinkled her nose at the memory of his boxers in her hands.

"Kim!" Ava and Mark hissed in unison.

"Alright, alright! I'll get to the point." She took a deep breath. "We went to the boat rentals and talked to Deloris," she said snidely. "Whom Ava paid two hundred bucks to… I might add," she said, shooting her a disapproving look.

Mark made a sound in his throat. "What Kim is getting at; is we took the boat out on the lake. Ava found the vilest smelling garbage you can ever imagine." He looked at Abbi. "Your daughter kicked it at my head!"

"I did not!" Ava shouted. "I merely just sent it flying… your way."

"Yeah… lucky for you, the meat was on the floor. If that had splattered on me, we both would have gone for a swim."

Abbi was getting more confused by the minute. Closing her eyes and counting to ten she held her hands up. "Hold it. Would someone mind getting to the damn point of all this?"

Kim took a deep breath. "Okay, here it is. In the garbage pail, there was a pack of rotten hamburger… hence the smell. On the package was this…"

She pulled the note out of her pocket, triumphantly holding it up for them to see.

"Written in what I … or…. we think… was the blood from the meat, and the same blood used for the note from the flowers."

Ben slipped his arm around Abbi as he took the note from Kim. With their heads together, they read the message.

"So, whoever this guy is, he's not only after you two but he's also after Raven Black." Kim gave a satisfied nod. Turning, she gave high fives to Mark and Ava. "Hey, maybe we should team up and become P.I.'s. Yeah?" She grinned, nodding at them.

Ben looked at Abbi. She read the self-doubt in his gaze.

"Go ahead. Tell them what you came up with." She encouraged him. She had a hard time believing his theory. But she knew she trusted him more than anyone in the room.

"Um, that sounds like a possibility, but...." He removed his arm from around Abbi's waist and walked to the table. Taking the laptop, he turned it around. "Look familiar, Mark?"

Mark walked over to stare at the screen. "That's Raven Black," he nodded, tapping the screen.

"Right," Ben said, sitting it down. He grabbed the yearbook. "Now look at... him." Ben stabbed the photo of Roland Eddy.

Mark looked at the page, his mouth agape, brows rose in surprise. "No! There's no way, man! That can't be!" Following Ben's thinking, Mark was horrified.

Ben nodded. "Yes, that's exactly what I'm thinking."

"What are you two going on about?" Kim asked. Frustrated, she took the book from Ben. "Who are you talking about?" She looked to Ben.

"That guy right there!" Mark pointed.

"You mean Roland Eddy?" She looked at Ben with an arched brow.

"Yeah," Mark responded. He looked at Ben. "You know, I always thought something was off with that guy. Man, I don't believe this," he said throwing up a hand.

"I'm not following," Ava frowned.

"Hey, Abbi, wasn't this the guy that sent you flowers and you threw them away?" Kim glanced at her questioningly.

"Yeah... I did," she stared blankly. She'd forgotten all about that. He had them delivered to her in a beautiful crystal vase.

Blood-red roses, twelve to be exact. She thought their dad had sent them for their mom. But that hadn't been the case. When she found out they were for her, she promptly threw them in the garbage. She didn't want to encourage any attention from him. She never mentioned it, nor did he. She liked him as a person, but that was as far as that went.

"Will someone please fill me in on what the hell is going on?" Ava demanded.

Ben looked at Ava and pointed to the computer screen. "This guy wanted my role for your mom's book." He pointed to the yearbook that Kim held. "And that guy. Roland Eddy, that went to school with her, is the same guy."

Now Abbi knew what Ben was about to say earlier. He hadn't finished his sentence when they had heard the knock on the door. She cleared her throat. "Am I correct in assuming," she looked at Ben. "Raven Black was mad you got the part without auditioning?"

He nodded in response.

"And now he's here, to make sure you can never take another one away from him again?"

Ben looked up; he thought a moment. "Yeah… I think it's more than just making sure I'm out of the picture."

Taking a hold of her shoulders, he lowered his voice. "Abbi, it's more than that. He wants you. The phone calls, the flowers, and the note." He rubbed her arms.

"The break-in," he softly reminded her. "Me…" He pursed his lips in indifference. "I'm just an inconvenience. One that would better suit his agenda, if I was out of the way for good."

She shook her head. *No, it couldn't be, that was absurd.*

"Mom, did you think to look at the video when Ben's drugs were delivered?" Ava asked. "Maybe the guy was stupid enough to bring them himself," she suggested.

"Why the hell didn't we think of that?" Ben asked Abbi, his eyes brightening. Smiling, he turned to Ava. He grabbed her by the arms. "Ava I could kiss you."

She closed her eyes tight. Bracing herself, she squeaked. "Please don't."

Ben laughed as he promptly smacked a loud kiss on her forehead.

"Hey, what about me?" Kim asked, pointing to her face. He took her by the arms and promptly kissed her on the forehead too.

She let out a soft sigh. "I need to find a man like that," she said, giving Mark a side glance.

He held up his hands. "No, no, no. You're way too much of a woman for me."

"Damn straight I am. I would eat you for a snack," she snorted.

Dropping a quick kiss on Abbi's lips, Ben tugged on her hand. "Come on love, let's go check out the video." Turning to the rest of them standing there awkwardly, he raised his brows and asked, "Aren't you guys coming?"

They all hurriedly followed Ben into Abbi's room. Abbi pulled out the laptop in the drawer, put in her password, and searched for the date.

"Who answered the door when they came?" she asked, eyes fixed on the screen.

Kim raised her hand. "That would be me."

"Did he look familiar at all to you?" Abbi asked.

"Not really. I wasn't paying much attention though." She made a disgusted look. "I was too busy staring at the shitty flowers he was handing me."

"Around what time was that?" Mark asked.

"Well, it was after supper, so I would say around seven," she answered with assurance.

Abbi typed in the search button for the time. The screen jumped to it immediately; they waited and watched as the video played on the screen.

"What was he driving?" Ben looked at Kim.

"Hmm, now that you mention it... he was walking. At the time I thought nothing of it."

Abbi sped up the recording a bit. She was going to click the mouse again when Mark pointed at the screen.

"There!" he said.

They all leaned in to get a better view. A man was walking, glancing around as if he was searching for someone. In his hands he carried something, as he cut across the front yard, making a beeline for the house. Climbing the steps, he crossed the porch and rang the doorbell.

Abbi sat transfixed. Staring at was what was in his hands. A small white bag and twelve long-stemmed roses bruised and beaten by the looks of them.

"That's him!!" Kim yelled. "That asshole lied to me; he had the flowers the whole time!"

"Precisely!" Ben said grimly.

"Man, you have skills! I don't know how you figure all this stuff out. Every damn time, too!" Mark said, smacking Ben on the back.

"So now what do we do?" Ava asked. "Do we call the police?"

Ben looked at Abbi. He noticed she was withdrawing into herself again.

"I'll call my brother, with any luck he can come here and help us figure it out," Mark answered Ava.

Ben gave Mark a pointed look, tilting his head in Abbi's

direction.

Glancing at Abbi, Mark followed his hint. Shooting his eyes to Ben, he gave him a nod.

"Great, but what do we do now?" Ava asked again.

Draping an arm around both Ava and Kim, Mark guided them to the door. "Right now, we take the boat back and leave these two alone," he said, with a jerk of his head.

***

Oh, my darling Abbi, I just know that we will be perfect together! I WILL mend your broken heart... silly girl falling for Ben in the first place was your one flaw. But I can overlook that. I just need you to leave the safety of your home. Seeing how you somehow blocked my number... I can't call you, now can I. ... Nor can I walk up to your door just yet. No... that wouldn't do at all...

Chapter 12

Ben closed the laptop with a snap. He knelt before Abbi, taking her cold hands in his. She was still sitting there, transfixed, lost in her thoughts.

"Abbi. Look at me," he whispered.

She looked down at him and saw the love shining from his eyes. She lifted her hand to run the backs of her fingers gently along his jawline. She thought back to when he was lying on the bed at the clinic, so pale against the whiteness of the sheets. She felt so helpless and guilty at the same time… But not this time, she thought. This time she was mad and getting madder by the minute.

Ben saw the anger building in her eyes. He saw the fire coming back. "We've got this, love," he said. Standing up, he tugged on her hands. "Come on. It's dark out. Let's go for a walk."

"Do you think that's a good idea?" she asked, with concern.

"I do. Yes. It's a beautiful night out. We'll just go in the backyard." Giving a sharp whistle he called for the dogs. Abbi snatched up a blanket from the window seat as they headed to the door. The dogs scrambled into the room, each one trying to be first out the door.

They made their way along the porch, down the steps to the middle of the yard. Ben took the blanket from her. Unfolding it, he spread it on the ground. "Sit, my love," he said softly.

Abbi sat, looking around. The light from the full moon bathed the yard with its glow. She patted the spot beside her. "Join me?"

"You need not ask me twice," he grinned, settling himself beside her.

"Ben, what are we going to do?"

"Shh, not tonight. Tonight, let's just forget the world," he murmured to her softly.

Nodding, she laid her head on his shoulder. She just had to know though. Frowning, she looked at him. "But what if...."

His mouth on hers cut her questioning off. Cupping her head in his hands, he deepened the kiss, as he laid her gently back on the ground. His other hand searched her body with an urgency. His hand reached for the hem of her shirt. Finding it, he touched her warm skin.

Shuddering from the touch of his hand, Abbi pulled the snaps of her blouse free. She lay there in her bra under the moonlight as Ben raked his eyes over her.

God, I'll never tire of her beauty... He wanted nothing more than to make love to her right there, but not for the world to see. He trailed a row of kisses from her belly button to her lips. He gave her one last plundering kiss before trailing his lips to her ear. "Not here, love," he murmured huskily. He put his arm under her knees the other around her back, lifting her. She wrapped her arms around his neck as he headed towards the house. His mouth never leaving hers.

Taking a breather, Abbi leaned back, "Ben put me down, it will be faster if I walk," she giggled, looking up at him.

He stopped in his tracks. His gaze dropped to her lips. Slowly, he bent his head to touch them again. "You're right," he said as he tore his mouth away to set her down.

"Come on," she grabbed his hand, leading the way back to her bedroom.

The dogs were all waiting, dashing in as she opened the door.

"We forgot the blanket," Ben said as he dropped her hand.

"Don't worry about it." She tugged his hand. She stopped, an idea forming in her mind.

"On second thought. Maybe it's better if you did, do you mind?" she asked. *It will give me some time to get ready...*

"Sure, be back in a second," he said, taking off out the door.

Abbi rushed into the bathroom. Pushing down the plunger, she twisted the taps to fill the tub, dumping a generous amount of Epsom salts and bubble bath in. She turned to light the candles scattered around the room.

Ben wasn't back yet. Walking to the door she opened it, looking to see if she could see him. There he stood, folding the blanket, staring out across the lake. Relieved, she went back to the bathroom, stripping her clothes as she did, leaving a trail for him to follow.

Ben was looking to see if there were any lights across the lake. Seeing nothing, he started back towards the house. When he and Abbi were out here, he had the feeling of being watched. Turning, he headed back to Abbi's room. Opening the door, he walked into silence. *Huh. Is she already sleeping?* Tossing the blanket on a chair, his foot caught on something. Looking down he saw Abbi's shirt laying there. A few feet away, her pants lay where she had kicked them off. His brows raised at seeing her panties lying a few feet further. Rounding the corner at the closed bathroom door, he found her bra wedged between the door and the frame. He slid the pocket door open, his breath catching in his throat at the sight before him. There she was, lounging in the tub. Her head was resting against the back... her hair falling over the edge. He slowly walked towards her. Her eyes were closed as the whirring of the jets slowly churned the water.

Bathed in candlelight, her skin glistened. The heady scent of jasmine in the air mingled with the bubbles that barely covered her breasts was intoxicating to him. He stood silently. He wanted to dip his head to suck on one nipple, just one, bringing her to dizzying heights of pleasure with his tongue.

She must have sensed him there for she opened her eyes.

Smiling at him, her voice thick with desire. "Hey handsome, care to join me?"

Images of doing just that flashed through his mind. He felt like jumping in fully clothed, taking her in his arms and giving her a pleasure so intense like she had never known before. He grabbed the neckline of his shirt, pulling it over his head. He rolled it into a ball, whipping it to the floor. Her eyes never left his body. He could feel the heat from her gaze scorching a path over his skin.

She reached out to touch him. Taking a step back, he waved a finger at her.

"Uh uh."

He reached for the waist of his jeans. Unbuttoning them, he slowly pulled the zipper down, gazing into her eyes, seeing them go from hot to fiery in a single heartbeat.

I should have thought this through a bit more... she thought, catching her teeth with her bottom lip. She was to be seducing him... and here he was doing it to her. She loved watching his muscles ripple under his skin. She so wanted to touch him, any part of him, she'd be happy with. But he denied her. He'd rather torture her... making her watch as his hands slowly undid his jeans. Her eyes followed as they dropped to the floor in a heap.

He stood there for a second, just watching her watch him.

Abbi licked her suddenly dry lips. The excitement building up in her made her wonder if it would always feel this way with him... as if every time was the first time.

Her heart was racing as she watched him pull his boxers down. Her eyes went immediately to his erection. *Good, God! Can one have an orgasm from just looking?*

Ben cleared his throat loudly. "Abbi?" He held his hand out to her. She didn't take it. She just kept staring at him. "Love?"

He took a step closer to the tub, putting his hands on the side of it, he leaned down looking into her eyes.

She looked at him then. Smiling softly, she said, "Hi."

"Hi yourself," he said, placing a soft kiss on her lips. He deepened it, his lips clinging to hers as he climbed into the tub, pulling her to him as he leaned back.

She wrapped her arms around his neck, laying on his hard body. She was fighting a battle within herself. She desperately wanted to mount him, but she also wanted this moment to last forever.

Tearing her mouth from his, she slowly backed away. She needed to distance herself or the wantonness in her would win. Looking him in the eyes, she saw the desire replaced with confusion.

What is going on with her? One minute she is more than willing and the next she is backing away as if she is... bored? "Did I do something wrong?" he asked her.

In answer, she ducked her head under the water.

Great, she's bored!

Abbi came up sputtering, wiping the water from her eyes.

"Are you going to answer me?" Ben asked, wondering how she could turn off like that so quickly.

"Yeah. It's simple really," she paused, running her foot along his leg to his inner thigh. "You drive me insane. I can't control myself around you." She ran her foot up his abs to his chest.

"Really?" The desire sprang back into his eyes.

"Yes. Really." She frowned. "You make me feel like a wanton sex-craved…"

She couldn't finish her words because his hand snaked out,

taking her foot. He brought it to his lips, lightly kissing the inner arch, trailing kisses up to her ankle along her calf. He lowered her leg into the water. Guiding it around his waist, he did the same with the other as he pulled her by the waist to him. Their slick bodies pressed together. His hot breath fanning over her already heated skin. She sucked in a breath when she felt his teeth nip her neck, followed by his tongue.

Breathing heavily, he murmured against her neck. "And you don't think you do the same to me?"

Abbi couldn't control it any longer. The thought of their lower bodies so close to each other. His lips… his hot breath…. his teeth on her skin, all had her shuddering a release. She held tightly to him, moaning her pleasure. She was just coming back to her senses when he grabbed hold of her hips lifting her. Slowly he eased into her warmth. She gasped at the sensation of him filling her. Raking her nails across his back, she arched her head as his lips scorched a trail along her throat. She shoved her hands into his hair, holding onto his head as it dipped to one nipple, slathering it with his tongue. *Good Lord, I feel like ripping his hair out…*

She was feeling so many emotions at that very moment that she was unsure what to do; he had her frozen. She moved her hands to his shoulders, bracing herself, she slowly raised her hips. Tightening herself around him, she silently sent a thank you to the Gods that be, that all those Kegels had worked. She lowered herself onto him, a millisecond later, she just about shot up and out of the water when his shaft encountered… "Oh. My. God," a guttural groan escaped past her lips, as a mixture of such intense pleasure and pain shot through her body.

So that's the g spot…

She panted as Ben took hold of her hips. Lifting her, just to slam her down on his shaft again and again, had them soaring ever closer to the edge of the universe. Water sloshed over the sides of the tub in time to their lovemaking. with one final thrust, he joined their lips, swallowing her groan of pleasure to join his.

He held her as she collapsed in his arms. He could feel her shaking. *Is she going to cry every time we make love?*

"Sweet one, are you okay?" he asked. Concern had him leaning back, searching her face.

She looked at him, smiling, a bubble of laughter escaping past her swollen lips. "See what you *do* to me?" she asked, laughing as she wrapped him in her arms.

"God, I love you woman," he smiled, nuzzling her neck.

She leaned back, placing her hand on his face, looking into his eyes. He could see the love there for him.

"I love you too. More than you will ever know." She softly kissed him on the lips. She sat back looking around the tub. One lone candle still proudly burned, casting low shadows on the walls, the rest, snuffed out from the waves in the tub. Thank goodness she had a drain installed in the floor. Untangling herself from Ben, she stood up and felt him watching her. She looked down at him and saw again, desire in his eyes.

Ben had to resist the urge to run his hands over her body when she emerged like a nymph from the water. It didn't surprise him when he felt the quick flare, rush to his cock again. She had that much power over him and she didn't even know it. Living without her would be impossible, he knew that. After this business with Raven Black, he'd ask her to move in with him. The problem was, the way he traveled all over the world, would she want to?

Abbi climbed out of the tub, crossed the room, and grabbed two fluffy bath towels from the shelf. She wrapped one around her head and the other around her body. Taking another one, she turned to Ben. He was watching her every move, a thoughtful look on his face.

"Isn't the water getting cold?" she asked, shaking out the folds in the towel. She held it up for him to step into.

"It is," he nodded. Placing his hands on the side of the tub he pushed himself up. He took the towel, wrapping it around his waist, as he stepped out of the tub.

Abbi was standing at the vanity, brushing her hair.

"Abbi?" He walked up to her, placing a soft kiss on her shoulder, he looked up at her reflection.

"Mhm?" she answered back, catching his eyes in the mirror.

He stood for a minute, his lips pressed to her skin, not sure he knew how to ask her.

She laid the brush down, turning to him. She put her hand on his chest. He was scaring her. "What is it?" Panic rose in her voice.

"When this is all over..." He paused.

What does he mean by 'this'...?

He saw the panic in her eyes. "No... God no! I didn't mean *us!*" he said, taking her into his arms. "I meant this deal with Raven Black..."

She took a steadying breath. *Thank God! I would have had to take drastic measures...* Picturing in her mind where she could tie him up so no one could find him... *I couldn't do that, or could I?...* She shook her head frowning. "Then what is it?"

"Would you want to move in with me at the point?" He asked, biting his lip. "We can build on... a bathroom just like this," he said, glancing around.

She walked to the tub and flipped the drain lever. She was not expecting this at all! She couldn't deny that she didn't think about the possibility that someday, if they were still together, they might. She was sure once he left for filming, he'd find someone else.

But if that didn't happen then they might live together, but this soon?

She bent to pick up his clothes. Tossing them over her shoulder, she walked into her bedroom. She stopped and looked at Ben. "What would I do with my house?" she asked, picking up her bra.

Rubbing his ear, he said, "Uh... I didn't think of that, to be honest."

She seemed unusually preoccupied with their clothes; he noticed. That was the third time she folded his jeans. *Ah... I get it, she's worrying again about us...* Walking to the bed, he dropped his towel and said, "We can discuss this more tomorrow. Abbi, love... put down the clothes." He pulled the sheets back and crawled into the bed. "Please come to bed?" he asked, holding the sheet for her to join him. She tossed his jeans onto the pile and marched over to her dresser.

"What exactly are you doing?" he chuckled.

Pulling out an oversized t-shirt and a pair of granny panties, she looked at him and said, "I'm getting dressed," she stated. "I can't sleep in the raw." *How has he not noticed that by now?*

"... what if a spider crawls," She stammered for the right word, "... you know, up there?" She motioned with her hand.

He threw his head back, a howl of laughter escaping past his lips. "I promise you; I won't let any spider crawl up there." His eyes shone with amusement.

She giggled, "How can you possibly promise that?".

"Come here, and I'll show you, love," he said softly.

She went to the bed and climbed in. Lying flat on her back, she pulled the covers up to her chin. She raised her brows, looking at him expectantly. "Well? I'm waiting."

He reached across her, slipped his hand behind her back and

turned her to face him. "Here." He laid his other arm out for her to lay her head on. "I'll show you," he murmured.

He shouldn't have said it using that tone of voice. Her insides were turning into molten liquid again. Any moment she'd be dripping like a broken faucet. She scooted closer, laying her head on his bicep. She felt his knee nudge between her thighs sliding up reaching to the junction of her thighs.

"Oh my," she gasped.

He had created a barrier that no spider could ever pass. If one tried to, it would most definitely drown, anyway. Her eyes were getting heavy. She felt his lips brush hers as she fought to stay awake. His hand gently stroking her back, she heard him whisper as she drifted off, "Goodnight, my sweet one."

Ben laid there with Abbi, holding her in his arms. The soft rise and fall of her chest pressed against his, told him she was asleep.

He waited for ten minutes. Ever so carefully he kissed her forehead. Sliding away from her, he crawled out of the bed. He had hated to leave her alone in the bed, but he had to come up with a plan to fleece Raven out… before it was too late.

Chapter 13

Abbi woke with a start. She reached out for Ben, only to find the bed empty. Rolling over, she looked at the clock on the side table... 11:00 am. She never slept that late! She could hear voices coming from the other room. Frowning, she threw the covers back, swung her legs over the edge, and bounded to the bathroom.

"Any idea how we're going to lure him out?" Kim asked, frowning at Ben's chart. *What the hell is this gibberish?*

Ben had noted the timelines of Abbi's contact with Roland/Raven since grade school. At least the ones he'd known of. "You think he's been stalking her all this time? While he was acting, even?" She asked skeptically.

He put his hands on his hips. "Yeah. He started in the 8th grade. I searched through Abbi's old yearbooks." He selected one out of the dozen that lay on the table; all the years Abbi attended school. Stepping close to Kim, he held it in his hands. Pointing to the 'Autograph' section, he said, "From what I could gather it started here." He read the entry... *"My dearest Abbi, I'll count the minutes until I see you again."* Cocking his head, he squinted. "They never dated, did they?"

"Oh, hell no! He wanted to. She shut him down every time. Good thing too, he's a psycho," she laughed.

Abbi breezed into the kitchen just then. "Hey you two." Putting an arm around Ben's waist, she reached up and kissed him.

"Morning Abbi," Kim mumbled, distracted. She was trying to

figure out what their next plan of action should be.

"Morning, love. You slept well; I trust?" He asked with a sexy grin.

Nodding, she smiled, "I did."

She walked to the cupboard and grabbed a mug. Pouring coffee into it, she asked, "Where are your partners in crime, Kim?" She added sugar and cream and raised expectant eyes at her sister. "Kim? Where are Mark and Ava?" she asked.

"Oh! ... They went to Mack's, seeing if he heard anything." Kim drummed her nails on the table. "Say, Abbi. Would you be bait?"

"Pardon me?" Abbi looked at with huge eyes.

"Like hell, she will!" Ben snarled.

Kim raised her hands defensively. "Relax! It was just a thought."

Intrigued and ignoring Ben's outburst. Abbi asked, "Bait as in how?"

Kim looked between her sister and the man she loved. There was no way she was getting in the middle of that. They were standing ten feet from her, staring at each other, but she could feel the tension mounting between them. *Hell, to the no!*

"Out with it, Kim," Abbi said, never taking her eyes from Ben's.

Ben stared Abbi down. "Don't you dare Kim," he said, menacingly.

"Uh, would you look at that! My phone is buzzing my boob at this very moment." Reaching into her bra, she produced her phone. Bringing it to her ear, she slowly made her way to the door.

"Ava! Sure, I can meet you guys at the store. Be right there!" She stuffed it back in her bra, desperately trying to escape out the door.

"Gotta go, guys," she waved, slamming it behind her. Whew! She had no idea where Ava and Mark were, seeing how she had been talking to air. As she set off across the yard, she thought how lucky it was that neither Abbi nor Ben had noticed her phone was upside down.

"Abbi, you're not putting yourself in harm's way," Ben said softly, leaning back against the counter, watching her drink her coffee. "I won't allow it." He folded his arms across his chest.

Abbi spit her coffee out. "Excuse me?" she wiped her mouth on her sleeve. "Did you just say you wouldn't allow it?" she questioned.

"Yeah. I did." He nodded his head. "Do you have a problem with that?"

Her eyes flashed daggers at him, "You're damn right I do! Do you have a better idea?" She calmed down when she realized he was only concerned for her safety and not trying to give her orders. "Honestly, this is getting old. It's been going on far too long," she said, looking down at the floor, sighing

Ben immediately felt like an ass. "Love... I'm sorry." Reaching to take her hand. He pulled her to him, holding her in his arms. "I don't want him even breathing the same air as you do. Do you understand that?"

She nodded, tears springing to her eyes. She felt so helpless. "What if I was with Mark?" She looked up at him. "Maybe seeing him with me will bring him out?" she suggested. She could tell he was weighing the possibility that it might work. "And if his brother is with us, even better."

He slowly nodded. "Yeah. I guess."

"You can come too, just wear a disguise, right?" she suggested.

"Yes. It might work."

She broke free from his embrace to pace the floor. "I know! I will throw a party! A huge BBQ and invite everyone from the village." She stopped. Pointing at him. "You most definitely will fit in with a disguise!"

He went to her. "Yeah, this could work, for sure." If anything happened to her, he wouldn't hesitate to kill Raven. "I'll be watching you from afar. You just make sure you're never alone," he said softly, catching her chin in his hand. He rubbed his thumb across her bottom lip.

"I won't be." She kissed his thumb before turning on her heel to grab her phone. Punching a number in, she brought it to her ear. Frowning, she lowered her cell and looked at it, "Dammit! I need to get a card."

Smiling, he handed her his. "Here, use mine."

"Thanks, babe," she grinned, dialing a number from memory.

"What are you doing now?" he chuckled.

She held up a finger to him. Smiling, she said into the phone, "Kim! Get your butt back here and bring Ava and Mark, too. We are going to throw a BBQ. Now please, get over here so we can plan it!" Hanging up, she turned to look at Ben. He was gone.

"Ben?" She walked towards the living room, pausing at the open French doors. He was standing out on the porch with his hands in his pockets, watching the dogs chase after a squirrel.

Abbi walked to him, laying a hand on his shoulder. Feeling him relax under her touch, she laid her head against his back. "This will work," she murmured.

He turned around to face her, his hands reaching to pull her close. "It better," he said, grabbing a fist full of her hair.

She pulled back, searching his eyes. Her own, softening as she saw the glisten of tears in his. "Hey, what is it?" she said, tears springing to her own.

He shook his head, licking his lips, he replied unconvincingly. "Nothing."

She took his face in her hands. "Ben. Tell me… please."

He wrapped his arms around her tighter and swallowed the lump in his throat. "Abbi. I swear to God… If something happens to you, it will be the end of me…" He dipped his head, kissing her with such sadness.

She felt like her very soul was being ripped from her body. The tears slipped down her cheeks; she couldn't help it. She knew what he was feeling… all too well. He leaned his forehead against hers.

"Love. If he touches one hair on your head. With God as my witness, I will kill him."

She was scared, not because she worried about herself, but because she knew he'd follow through. She shook her head. "Shh! Don't think like that. Nothing will happen. I'll play you off as my new boyfriend… Sven." She smiled through her tears.

"Hey… hey… hey! Let's get this party planned!" Mark yelled from the side yard as the trio rounded the corner.

Filing onto the porch, Ava noticed immediately her mom had been crying. *Has Ben been bitching her out?* From what Kim had said, they had been on the verge of a fight when she left. She looked at Ben. She was shocked to see him just as upset as her mom, noticing the redness of his eyes.

God, this must be so hard for them both. "Mom, Ben, are you guys okay?" she asked.

Ben gave a brief nod, not saying a word.

"Yeah, we're okay, honey," Abbi said, hugging her. "I'm just happy you're all here," she said, looking around at her family, which now included Mark.

Kim was relieved they had worked things out between them. She rushed to Abbi, hugging her. "We got this, baby girl," Kim whispered into her hair.

Pulling away she said, "Soon you and your man here…" she jerked a thumb at Ben, "… will be so bored for lack of excitement, you won't know what to do with each other," she laughed.

Ben snickered. "Uh, I doubt that."

Kim shook her head. Would she ever stop sticking her foot in her mouth? "Wrong choice of words!" She turned to go into the house. "Damn. I need to find a man like that."

Everyone took her cue, and followed her into the house.

"My brother is on his way, as we speak." Mark raised his brows up and down at Kim. "I could set you two up on a date."

"Does he have an accent and look like a Greek god," Kim asked, seriously.

"Nope. But he's a cop," Mark offered.

"Hmm." She nodded her head, "I'll consider it," she stated, cackling. "Hah…. I crack myself up." Pulling out a chair, she sat. "Okay, enough of this crap. Let's plan," she said, folding her hands on the table.

"How many people are we talking?" Ava asked, pulling out a notebook from the drawer.

"Everyone from the village," Abbi said, sitting down.

"Everyone?" Mark asked. "Don't you think that's a little too much?"

"No. I want Roland or whatever he calls himself, to feel like he's welcome to come. The more people here, the more likely that will happen."

"That is true," Ava said, writing it down.

"What about Ben? What are we going to do about him?" Kim asked.

"Well, I thought we would disguise him." Abbi bit her lower lip. "I don't know how, though."

"Well, you could put a dress on him and call him granny." Kim smacked the table, laughing at the visual her joke made.

"Or we could just put a wig and hat on him," Mark suggested. He looked at Ben. "I think there are some costumes in the attic over at your place."

"All I know is that I will be beside Abbi all day, or at least try to be," Ben stated. Taking her hand in his, he brought it to his lips.

"You guys make me sick," Kim said. "If you two ever break up. You know where to find me," she smiled wickedly at Ben.

"That will never happen," they both responded in unison.

"Damn it!" Kim muttered, frowning.

Ava spoke up. "Well, I for one, am thrilled for the both of you," she said looking to them. "Ben, I seriously had doubts about you. But after getting to know you, I realize you're cool." She came around, standing behind his chair to hug him.

"Hey now, don't be doing that!" Mark said.

"Jealous, are you?" Ava asked mischievously.

"Me... Why would I be jealous?" he scoffed.

"Thanks, Ava." Ben looked at Abbi. "I think I speak for both of us, that it means a lot."

"It does... more than you know," Abbi said, squeezing her daughter's hand as she walked back to her chair.

"So, we'll run to Mack's and spread the word... grab the food while we are there. Is there anything else we need?" Kim asked, looking around the table.

Everyone shook their heads no.

"Great. In two days, this shindig will be good to go." Standing up, she said to Ava and Mark. "Let's go, you two."

They got up, pushing their chairs in. Mark looked at Ben. "I'll bring the wig and hat over later tonight," he offered.

"How about we just walk over there when you guys get back?" He looked at Abbi for confirmation.

"Do you think it's wise?" she asked. She didn't want to chance Ben being spotted.

"Yeah. It will be dark. Besides, I don't know about you, but I'm getting a bit stir crazy, myself." He sighed, standing up to follow the others to the door.

"Yeah, I am too," she had to admit.

"It's settled. We will pop by later."

Ben held the door open for them. "Give me a ring when you get back, will you Mark?"

"Will do, buddy!"

Ben stood watching them for a bit, the same thing kept running through his mind. *This better work...* He feared if it didn't, he would lose Abbi for good...

Chapter 14

Ben raised his hand to knock on the door, the other held onto Abbi's. The dogs were running, noses to the ground, sniffing every nook and cranny that they could.

Abbi glanced down at the porch, noticing the bloodstain had disappeared. She tugged on Ben's hand, getting his attention. She pointed to the floor.

"It's gone."

"Huh, I wonder…"

The opening door interrupted his words as he glanced up. Mark stood there and noticed Abbi looking at the porch floor.

"Yeah, there was some leftover paint in the shed," he said. "Had to do a couple of coats, but it's good as new now. Oh! I painted around your BBQ too," he said, smiling.

Ben's face lit up. "Thanks, man. I was wondering if I could get the paint to match," he said, as they crossed the threshold.

"You know this is your house, man… why did you knock?" Mark asked, laughing.

"No idea. I guess I've just been at Abbi's so much lately, it felt wrong not to."

Kim came in from back patio door. "Hey, guys. Nice night out there for a stroll," she said.

"It is that," Abbi agreed, nodding.

"I never came across it, so where is the attic?" Ben asked.

"Come on," Mark said, waving his hand for Ben to follow.

Abbi stood looking around the house, catching every detail that she missed before.

She loved it, always had. But could she see herself living here now that she had made her house a home?

"What are you looking for, Mom?" Ava asked.

She spun around on her heel, looking to her daughter, sitting at the table. "Um... nothing. Just looking at the house," she said.

Looking up at the ceiling, Abbi frowned. There was a walkway directly above her. *How in the world did I miss that before?* ... She nodded her head towards it. "How do you get to that?"

Ava and Kim swung their heads to look up.

"Oh, that's the hallway upstairs. The staircase is in the front foyer," Ava said, writing in a notebook.

"What?" Abbi blinked rapidly. She pointed to the door that she and Ben just came in.

"Is that not the front?"

"Nope, I'll show you."

Abbi followed Ava through to the living room, the same room that she thought was the back room the guys went to. Kim was taking up the rear.

"Wow, this place is a lot bigger than I realized."

True she had only seen the kitchen, laundry room, and the bathroom before, and of course Ben's bedroom, but still. It just went on and on.

They climbed the stairs to the second level. To the left at the top was a room with a drop-down staircase.

Ava jerked her head. "That's where the guys are, and this way... is the master and spare bedrooms." She turned to the right and headed down the hallway.

Waist-high glass sides allowed a view to the lower level. She looked over the edge to see the kitchen and dining area below.

She was falling more in love with it with every step she took.

Could I live here? Maybe the better question to ask is, should I live here...

They came to the end. A door to the right stood open, revealing a medium-sized bedroom with windows facing the lake. Straight ahead, they stepped into the master bedroom. She raised her brows when she saw it. The king-sized bed was breathtaking. The bed itself was high off the floor. Steps led up to it on the sides and the foot; as if it was on a pedestal. It was something that one would see in a castle it was so grand... almost over the top.

"Ben asked me to move in with him..."

"What?!" Ava looked at her, shocked.

"Mhm," she nodded. Yeah, she could see herself living here. As much as she loved the bed, it would have to go though. Her luck, she'd roll out of it and crack her head open on the stone.

"Well, are you?" Kim asked. "What will you do with your place if you do?"

Abbi sighed. "Not sure to be honest to both of your questions."

She walked over to the windows. Just like the other bedroom, there was a wall of them overlooking the lake. Unlike the other room, these went from floor to ceiling.

"Do the windows open?" She looked at Ava.

She knew her mom would love them the minute she saw them. Walking over to a picture on the wall, she slid it over to reveal a panel. Pressing a button, she smiled. "They sure do."

Abbi was in love. She could feel the warm breeze on her heated skin. Yes, she could see herself living here. She was lost in thought, still gazing out the window when two strong arms wrapped around her waist, pulling her back against a chest of steel.

"What are you thinking about love?" he murmured near her ear.

Nuzzling her neck, he felt her grow tense in his arms. "Don't worry sweets. I sent them downstairs."

It amazed her how he could read her so well.

Relaxing, she tilted her head, thrilled at the touch of his mouth. She gave a blissful sigh. "I think I love the house almost as much as I love the owner." She grinned at his approving growl.

"Oh really? Well, I heard the owner is… you know… an ass." His lips spread a blazing trail to the sensitive spot just behind her ear.

"Yes, the owner has a nice ass." she laughed at the memory of that conversation. Turning to face him, she said, "As a matter of fact. The owner has a nice everything." She kissed the exposed skin of his chest where his shirt was open. Gazing into his eyes, she softly said, "The owner couldn't be more perfect to me if he tried."

"We all have flaws, Abbi. Not you of course, but the rest of us do," he said grinning down at her.

"Perhaps we're both a tad blinded, hmm?" She kissed him then. He felt perfect to her. No one had ever treated her so tenderly or made her feel so cherished in her entire life. Her husband, who had vowed to love her, showed revulsion at the sight of her scars and stretch marks. Yet this man saw past them, touched them as if they weren't even there. No, he was perfect. He was her rock in a sea of insanity.

Ben had to pull away from her, he wanted nothing more than to toss her onto the bed and make sweet…. No, that wouldn't do with the others downstairs. "So, what do you think?" he asked, putting some distance between them.

"I'm thinking this place is a lot bigger than I first thought," she chuckled.

"Yeah, it's big. But that bed…" He gave it a sneaky look.

"Uh-huh," she said. She didn't know what he thought of it, but the more she looked at it, the more she found it to horribly out of place. The bed itself was great, just not the rest of it.

He shook his head. "Sorry if you like it, Abbi, but it's gotta go."

"Thank God. I thought maybe you wanted to keep it. All I can picture is me…"

He swung his gaze to hers and raised a brow in question. "Falling and cracking your head on the steps?" At her nod, he smiled. "Right, that was the first thing I thought of too." He took her by the hand. "Okay, let me show you what I have in mind." He directed her to the spare bedroom.

"This is where I thought we could build a bathroom like yours," he looked at her for approval.

"We could put the tub here." He stepped in front of the windows. "… a corner tub though, big enough for the both of us." He threw her a sexy smile. "And the shower could go over there," he pointed to the opposite wall. "And in here…." He walked to the open door and flicked the light on, revealing a massive walk-in closet. "We could have the sink, toilet, and a towel closet." He folded his arms across his chest, smiling. She could tell he had thought about this for some time. "What do you think?"

"I think…" she paused, looking around.

He hurried on, "Or we could build on and redo a few rooms downstairs. You could have the master as a library/office… the windows in there would allow for natural lighting. Also, the breeze in there is amazing." He was rambling on, he knew. But she wouldn't say anything. He was readying himself for her flat-out refusal.

"Ben, whatever you think… its fine with me."

"Well, that isn't very helpful," he responded, the smile falling from his face.

"We could live in a train car for all I care, as long as we're together," she told him. "If you wanted to move back to England... say it and I'll start packing. I won't be happy about it, but I would leave in a heartbeat if you asked... that is if you wanted me to." *Shit! Maybe he wouldn't want me to...*

She, of course, had to think of that after the fact. "But just so you know. Where I go, so do my animals. If it means me having to hire a private plane so they can ride in first-class than that's what I'll do." She held her breath. She knew he loved the animals as much as she did, didn't he?

"I have no plans to move back to England, Abbi. This is where I want to be. With you and your animals. Either here or at your place, I don't care."

"Yes!" She was so happy, she jumped on him, wrapping her legs around his waist. Grabbing his head with both hands, she tilted it up to plant a wet kiss on his lips. She was so relieved. Not that she hadn't meant every word she'd said, but she didn't want to fly clear across the world. Unwinding her legs from his waist, she slid down him. She could feel the swell at the front of his jeans against her as her feet touched the floor. That thrill of excitement shot through her again, spreading like wildfire. "Let's go home," she said, holding out a hand.

"My sentiments exactly, love." He gave her a knowing smile, as he shut the lights off.

They were walking down the stairs when she stopped and turned to him, frowning. "What will I do with my house?" she bit her lip.

"Mark said he will rent it or buy it, whichever you want to do."

Shocked, she lowered her voice to a whisper. "Mark? You're kidding, right? He just sold this place to you and now he wants my place? Will he live in it though? I can't just leave it empty, as he did with this one."

"Yeah, he's determined… says he's a new man. Funny, but I believe him, this time."

Continuing down the stairs, she said, "OK. I'll ask him about it." She'd almost forgot the reason they were there. She glanced over her shoulder. "Did you get your disguise?"

"Sure did." He grabbed a clear plastic bag off the last step.

"Is that a… ponytail?" she wrinkled her nose as she stepped onto the floor of the front foyer. It looked like a dead squirrel that had seen better days.

He chuckled. "Yeah. I'm dressing like a biker. Think I'll pass?" He asked, sticking the wig on his head.

She waved a hand in front of her face. "Uh yeah. But that's gross. What is that smell?" she gagged.

"Mothballs," he answered grinning.

"Hey, you guys wanna join?" Kim called.

Mark and Ava were sitting on the couch while Kim was in a recliner. All three had their eyes glued to the TV.

"Thanks, but we are heading back," Ben answered.

"Suit yourselves."

As they were walking on the trail back to Abbi's house, she couldn't help but wonder what else was in the bag. Taking it from him. she asked, "What is the black leather looking thing?" It was too dark for her to tell.

"Oh. That's a vest," he said with a laugh. "You'll get to see my chest all day."

"Great!" *Awesome… All the women present won't be able to keep their eyes off him…* Just what she needed.

Ben put his arm around her shoulders. He knew that tone; the doubt was back, rearing its ugly head again. Why now? He had no idea. But one way or another he'd find out.

"So, Mark was telling me they spread the word about the party. Kim told Mack to tell everyone it was potluck. You okay with that?" he glanced her way, as they came into her yard.

"Yeah, it's fine. Mack will probably bring enough to feed a small army," she said with a shaky laugh as she went up to the steps to her house.

He nodded, and noticed her fumbling with the lock, "Want to tell me what's bothering you, love?" he asked, taking the keys from her trembling hand.

"Nothing, I'm fine…." At his glance, she added, "Really, I am." She tried desperately to act normal, she was failing miserably.

He looked at her, noticing her agitation. "Abbi…" He said her name in a deep warning voice as he pushed the door open. Letting her enter first he added, "I know when something is bothering you."

She went directly into the kitchen. She felt the sudden urge to clean something… anything. Picking up the animal dishes, she took them to the dishwasher. *Damn! He's got to be tired of my constant worrying that he will leave… Hell; I know I am!*

Biting her lip, she risked a glance in his direction. He stood there in the middle of the room, waiting for her to respond. Sighing, she finally said, "The same thing as usual…." She grabbed the detergent from under the sink, tossed a scoopful in and shut the door, setting it to on.

Turning to face him, she leaned her back against the counter, gazing down at the floor. "I don't want other women ogling you okay?" She looked up at him now. "Especially younger ones."

"Fair enough," he said, turning towards the hallway.

Fair enough? That was it? What the hell kind of answer is

that? "Where are you going now?"

Stopping, he turned to look at her.

"To bed... want to join me?" he murmured in that voice that always made her melt.

She stepped away from the counter, following him. "Fine... sometimes you're impossible, you know that, right?"

She just about collided into his back, he stopped so abruptly.

He turned and bent down, wrapping an arm around the back of her knees. He scooped her up onto his shoulder amid her gleeful laughter.

"Ben put me down!"

"Watch your head, love," he said, as he swung her around, heading towards her bedroom.

How can I watch my head when my eyes are looking at your glorious ass?

She felt herself being plopped onto the bed. Closing her eyes to the vertigo this man created, she felt him lay on the bed. His body spooning to her side. She opened one eye. There he was, his head propped on one hand, staring at her face intently, desire in those beautiful eyes.

"Hi. How you doing?" he murmured, raising a brow in question... a soft smile on his lips.

She was suddenly breathless. "Um, hi... good. You?"

He covered her legs with one of his. "Good, good," he said, grinding his lower body into her hip. "Fantastic actually," he murmured, inching his face closer to hers.

Whispering against her lips, "Now that that's settled..." His voice dripping with lust he added, "... Let me show you how impossible I can be." His lips soft at first intensified with every beat of her heart. She moaned, opening her mouth to his seeking tongue.

Ben couldn't get enough of her as she tugged on his shirt, pulling it from his jeans.

He broke free long enough to pull it over his head. His lips returned, blazing a trail to her neck, nipping her there. He felt the shiver of pleasure ripple through her body. Hearing her cry out his name when he moved away from her, caused his cock to pulsate.

She opened her eyes to see him staring at her with such an intensity; she thought she did something wrong.

"What?" she looked at him.

In answer, he reached for her shirt, slowly working each button loose, his eyes never leaving hers.

Abbi was about to go over the edge with just the look he cast her way. She shimmied out of her pants, as he continued to work the buttons. She was about to rip the damn shirt off when the last one let free. She lay there, in her bra and panties, waiting for his next move. Something was off. She was ready to jump his bones, and all he wanted to do was sit and... stare at her?

Ben was deliberately taking his time. He wanted this moment to last forever. He knew Abbi was champing at the bit, but she was just going to have to wait.... "Love, roll over," he murmured, using the tone that he knew drove her crazy.

She did as he asked. Propping her chin upon her arms, she waited. *What the hell is he doing?*

He saw her attempt to look over her shoulder at him. Placing a gentle hand at the back of her neck he said, "Uh uh, love."

She was getting weirded out and was about to tell him so when she felt his lips touch the back of one knee.

Ben gripped the waist of her panties, pulling them down as he laid soft kisses in a trail up her leg. Further, they traveled to her butt cheek, lightly nipping. He reveled as she sucked in a quivery breath when he darted his tongue to the spot, soothing the sting. He pulled her free of her underwear, his hands traveling up the backs of her legs.

Slipping between them at her thighs, his finger searching out the pearl he knew was there. His lips continued to travel upwards to the dimples at the small of her back, his tongue tracing the circles there, as his fingers found what they were seeking. He heard her soft moan; her legs clenched, trapping his hand. He inserted his thumb while his fingers lightly feathered her.

He could feel her insides tightening as he trailed his lips to her neck.

Abbi couldn't help but bite her lip as a moan escaped her throat. She just about ate the damn pillow she had been resting on when he'd slipped his thumb into her wetness, his fingers ever so softly teasing her even more. She felt his warm breath at the back of her neck as she rode his hand. His lips nuzzling her ear. *Dear God! This man is...* She couldn't even think of a word as he brought her to the edge of the universe.

Ben could tell she was close to climaxing. "Love let my hand go," he whispered hotly against her skin.

Is he crazy? She reluctantly did as he asked when his lips touched just behind her ear. She felt him kneel on the bed, spreading her legs with his knees. *There was no way she could....* She couldn't even formulate a thought.

Ben laid on top of her. "Are you, okay, love? I'm not too heavy, am I?"

Good Lord! NO! ... Her mind screamed. She couldn't even speak. Instead, she shook her head no vehemently. She laid there, loving the feeling of him draped over her.

His shaft felt like satin as he slowly entered her. That did it for Abbi. She was already soaring upwards in a dizzying, soul-shattering climax.

Ben waited until she was coming off the high. He knew she

Moonlit Stalker

needed to concentrate on the feelings she was feeling. When he felt her returning, he knelt and grabbed her by the hips. Jerking her upwards towards him, as he rammed forward. He bent over her back, his mouth finding her shoulder, nipping it. It blew Ben away... the sensations she stirred in him. He covered her breast with one hand, teasing the peak as the other splayed across her stomach.

Abbi turned her head towards him, her mouth seeking. He kissed her, swallowing her cry of ecstasy. She matched him stroke for stroke, as together they went over the edge. Unable to move; she had never felt so utterly spent in her life. Ben gathered her into his arms, pulling the blankets around them.

Abbi tilted her head up at him. She kissed him on the neck. "You're right. You are impossible," she whispered.

His gaze dropped to her lips, lightly touching them. "Am I now?" he murmured.

She felt like she was liquid. She could barely keep her eyes open, smiling she answered, "It was impossible to know your next move."

"Get some rest, my love." He chuckled; his arms tightened around her as they both drifted off to sleep.

Chapter 15

A party! Oh, how I love parties. My Abbi is throwing one just for me today! I must show up. Perfect timing too. You have to be well on the way of being over Ben. I must get ready for you, my sweet darling....

***

It was a beautiful sunny day with clear blue skies perfect for a BBQ with friends and family. Too bad there was a dark cloud hanging over it. Abbi kept scanning the crowd, wondering if Roland would show, as did the others.

True to his word, Ben was never more than ten feet from her. She gazed at him, thankful she had her shades on, otherwise she wouldn't have been able to do so, at least not as often as she liked. Her brow furrowed as she saw a girl a little too close to him for her liking. Her nerves were shot already… now, this… She looked at the redhead sizing him up. Any minute the girl would make her move. Would she be able to just stand by and watch? Ben must have seen her behind his shades. He quickly escaped, making a beeline to Ava, his ponytail swaying with every step. She breathed a sigh of relief. Thank God he wore a t-shirt under that vest; otherwise, she'd have to beat the women off. Hearing her name called, she spun around.

"Abbi, girl!" Mack said, approaching with a bowl in each hand.

"Mack! It's great to see you!" she said, taking the bowls from him to place on the already laden table.

"How're you doing?" he asked.

"I'm good," she nodded.

"You hear anything from Ben at all?" he asked, looking concerned.

"Ah... No, I haven't," she lied, setting the bowls down.

He shook his head, tsk-tsking. "That's too bad... I thought you two hit it off."

"Yeah. Well these things happen," she said with a sigh.

"Mack! How are you?" Kim asked, approaching from behind him. She held up her hand, "Before you answer that... Abbi, Mark needs you in the kitchen for a minute," she said, jerking her head towards the house.

"Oh?" Abbi frowned. "Oh! Right! ... Okay. I'll talk to you again soon, Mack. Enjoy yourself." She heard them talking about tourists as she hurried away.

Ben had to escape fast. If he'd stayed there, the redhead would have blown his cover. He couldn't go to Abbi, so he did the next best thing.

"Ava, hug me," Ben hissed close to her ear.

"What! Ew. No!" she turned to him, confused as hell.

"Redhead, six o'clock," he nodded.

She turned around to see which redhead he was talking about exactly.

"Don't look!!" he exclaimed, grabbing her by the arms. "That is Lorna Parker."

"So?" she raised her brows in question.

"The actress." At her blank stare, he continued. "If she gets too close to me, which she was, she'll recognize me."

Ava gave an exasperated sigh.

"Well, I couldn't very well go to Abbi, now could I? Just pretend we are together or something." he hurriedly said.

"Oh, God! Do I have to?" she griped.

"Yes!"

"Just so you know... I'm not enjoying this," she said, grimacing.

"Neither am I... Now will you get a grip, it will be over soon. Just do it quickly. Here she comes!" He wrapped her in his arms.

Kim was chatting to Mack, her eyes roaming the yard in search of Roland as she sipped her drink. She did a double take. "Holy *shit*!!!" she choked on her vodka and O.J.

What the hell? ... Who in God's name s Ava hugging?

"You okay, Kim?" Mack asked, smacking her on the back.

"Uh... yeah, Mack." She wheezed. "Just swallowed a bug... I think," she responded absently, watching Ava and the mystery man. She scrutinized them as the two parted, heading towards the house, the man flung his arm over Ava's shoulder... *That isn't a man. That's Ben! ...*

"Excuse me, Mack," Kim mumbled. Determined to find out what the hell was going on, she stalked after them.

"Abbi. Good, you're here." Mark smiled at her as she stepped into the kitchen. "This is my brother, Steve." He turned to the man beside him.

"Hi Abbi, nice to meet you." Steve held out his hand.

"Thanks for coming, sorry it's under these circumstances," she mumbled.

"No problem. Has there been any sign of Raven?" Steve asked, looking at them.

"I haven't seen him. But I don't know if I would even recognize him, to be honest. I saw him briefly about a month ago, wearing a hat and winter gloves, but I didn't get a good look."

Steve pulled something from a folder he was holding. "No worries. Here's a recent photo," he said, passing it to Abbi.

She scanned the photo. An older version of the boy she had once known stared up at her. She stood shaking her head.

"What is it?" Steve asked.

She looked up at him. "I just don't understand why. Why would he risk everything?" She passed the photo to Mark.

"Simple... He's infatuated with you. Has been for some time to my understanding?" He looked at Mark for confirmation.

"Yeah. Well, that's what we suspect anyway," Mark answered him.

Ava and Ben came into the house just then, with Kim hot on their heels.

"Hey, you two! Just what the hell was that?" She yelled, jerking her thumb towards the yard.

Ben walked to Abbi's side. "That was a public display of affection," he answered dryly, looking at Kim.

"What happened?" Abbi's eyes shot to his. *Was it Roland?* ...

"Lorna Parker is what happened," Ava supplied. "Ben made me hug him."

"Really?" Mark frowned.

Kim was waiting for the impact of Mark's fist to contact with Ben's jaw; it didn't happen.

"What the hell is she doing here?" Mark asked, sending Ben a quizzical look.

Ben shook his head. "No idea. But it can't be good."

"Hey, Ben." Steve nodded in greeting.

"Hey man. Thanks for coming," Ben said, holding his hand out.

Steve shook it, asking, "What exactly happened out there?"

"Wait... who is Lorna Parker?" Abbi asked, confusion on her face.

Mark was just about to speak when he caught Ben's slight shake of his head. Turning his head to the side, Mark gave Ben a dark look. "She has a right to know." Mark tried to reason with him.

Ben glared at him, knowing he was right. He turned to Abbi; his eyes immediately softened. He licked his lips. "Abbi. You saw the redhead who was coming towards me?"

At her nod, he continued. "Right. That is Lorna Parker. She and I dated, very briefly. Nothing happened between us... not that she didn't try." He watched the emotions play across her face, her tears springing to her eyes. He hated to continue, but he had no choice. "It upset her when I broke it off and she vowed to get me back."

Abbi didn't know what to do. Hearing those words was almost her undoing. "Excuse me," she mumbled, making a hasty retreat to the bathroom. All three dogs were lying on the floor, jumped when she slammed the door shut. Leaning back against it, she slumped to the floor in a heap, hugging her knees to her chest. Brutus came to her, resting his head on her knees, he let out a big sigh. "I'm a fool, boy. I knew this would happen, but did I listen to myself?" She muttered to him, burying her face in his fur.

Ben was more concerned with his ex being there than Raven, it seemed. *Did he secretly invite her? Why else would she go to him in a disguise of all things?* She jumped at the knock on the door. "Go away," she mumbled.

"Abbi open the door." It was Kim.

"No. Just go away!" she yelled.

"Oh, for cripes sake, Abbi, open the damn door," Kim yelled back.

"It's open," she sulked.

Kim turned the handle, pushing on the door to open it.

She found that it wouldn't budge more than an inch. "Move your ass!" she yelled.

Abbi scooted forward, sliding Brutus as she did. "That's as far as we're moving."

Kim shoved herself through the opening. Stumbling into the room, she almost fell flat on her face. "What the hell is wrong with you?" Kim asked, accusingly.

"Me? What's wrong with ME? His EX is back," Abbi hissed. "Don't you get it? She's here to win him back! I don't stand a chance," she said, shaking her head.

"How can you be a writer when you're that dumb?" Kim asked.

Abbi just stared at her.

"Do you honestly think he'd call his ex and have her come here to meet him? Give your head a shake, Abbi."

"What am I supposed to think?" Abbi glared at her as Lucy came, settling herself in her lap.

"Not that Abbi. The guy is crazy for you. How can you not see that?"

"It won't last you know," Abbi bit back. She laid her head on her knees. "He will find someone younger, someone, prettier…" she mumbled miserly.

"Will you fuck off with that age bullshit? Have you seen the women out there? He could have any of them, but no he chooses you! Someone who is giving herself a pity party on the bathroom floor! If he wasn't interested in you, why is he still here?"

Good question, why is he still here? She brought him nothing but grief since meeting her.

Kim squatted in front of her and reached a hand to lift Abbi's chin. Looking into her eyes, she said, "Ben is the best thing that has ever happened to you, aside from your kids, Abbi. Accept it, embrace it and most of all, be thankful you found each other." As she stood up, she added quietly. "Most people never find a love like that, don't let it go for God's sake." She offered her hand, Abbi took it. Standing up, she hugged Kim. "I've been an idiot," she sniffed.

"Nah," Kim scoffed as she turned the doorknob. "You're just crazy."

The dogs took off like rockets when she opened the door.

Kim jumped, with a laugh, "Oh! You scared the crap out of me."

Abbi looked around her to see Ben leaning against the wall... waiting for her. He smiled at Kim.

"Thanks," he said, stepping forward, hugging her.

"OH! All right! I'll gladly accept," Kim giggled, wrapping her arms around him.

He kissed her on the forehead, thanking her again as he let her go.

"Lord have mercy," she fanned a hand in front of her face. Looking at Abbi, she said, "Don't you screw this up." Turning, she held onto the wall as she headed back to the kitchen.

"Hi," Ben said, looking at her. He reached out a hand to stroke her cheek, slipping it to the back of her neck, as he pulled her to his chest.

"I'm sorry, I jumped to conclusions. I shouldn't have done that," she quietly said.

He breathed in her intoxicating scent, rubbing her back he said, "Abbi, I'm here because I love you. With every breath I take, I take it for you. Wild horses couldn't drag me away from you.... Please, stop doubting us."

She nodded. "I promise, no more doubts."

He kissed her, so tenderly she thought she'd start crying. Pulling back, he looked at her. "You know what? This wig has to go," he said, pulling it off.

"Ben, you can't. He will recognize you," she pleaded.

"He's already here, love. Mark told me Steve spotted him ten minutes before Kim opened the door."

"Even more of a reason for you to wear it," she reasoned.

"It's fine. I'm not hiding any longer. The cops are watching from a distance. Steve called in the local force. They're out on a boat, watching his every move."

She looked like she was ready to bolt.

"Abbi, nothing will happen to you. I'm here. He won't get within twenty feet of you okay?"

"It's you I'm worried about Ben. When he sees you, he's going to flip out."

"I hope he does," he said airily. "Sorry, it's been a long time coming. Steve and Mark have a plan. It's time I filled you in." He reached in his pocket, revealing a small box with a wire in his hand.

***

Abbi wasn't sure about this plan as she made her way into the backyard. For starters, she felt everyone could see the wiretap under her shirt.

Ben had put it on her, making sure it was well concealed. He explained that the police needed to hear Raven confess to anything that they suspected him of doing. She was to mingle among the crowd and never be left alone.

She scanned the faces there with every step, making her way slowly to the water's edge where the bar was.

***

Ben was standing at the side of the house. Brutus and Molly

stood by his side, bringing sticks for him to throw occasionally. He was to stay out of view until Steve gave him the signal. He wasn't entirely sure he could stay put. That would mean waiting until Abbi was over half a yard length from him. He was itching to make a mad dash to her right at this very moment. But no, he had to wait, going too early, could scare Raven off. But if he waited, it would mean he'd be out of reach to protect her if something went wrong. To hell with it, he was going. Calling the dogs to come, all three set off across the yard.

***

Abbi glanced around as she made her way towards the lake. She saw that most of the people were still here, all down by the water's edge. The closest person to her right now was Ben, and he was clear across the yard by the house. She had no idea where Raven was in the sea of people. She found it weird to even refer to him by that name, but the more she thought about it, the more he resembled the bird he so aptly named himself after. She could see the boat offshore where the police waited, ready to spring into action when the need arose. Steve and Kim were sitting at the fire pit, talking. Ava and Mark were over by the bar, talking to Lorna. Wait... *Why would they be talking to her?* Her foot caught on a tree root, hidden in the grass, causing her to stumble. Abbi felt a hand grab her from behind, catching her from falling flat on her face.

"Abbi, darling. Be careful," the unfamiliar man's voice cautioned.

Tightness gathered in her chest as she slowly turned around. *Oh God, did he feel the wired box under my shirt?* She felt the panic rising with every breath she took.

"Uh... I'm sorry. Have we met?" she asked, hoping she sounded unbothered despite her racing heart.

He seemed taken aback as if she should have known who he was. "Oh, don't play coy with me, darling. It's Roland. From high school. Raven Black, the actor now," he said, grinning like the fool he was.

"Oh! Roland! Yes! You have changed so much. I didn't recognize you." Her fake smile faltered.

"I just wanted to say, how sorry I am to hear about the passing of Ben Quinn."

He hurried to explain, "He was a colleague of mine. I knew he was a… friend of yours. It was bound to happen… just a matter of time. He should never have been cast for the lead role in your book."

***

Ben quickened his pace as he saw Raven approach Abbi from behind. Abbi, no! She just had to trip at that very moment for God's sake.

***

Abbi was floored that he would even mention Ben's name. "Who told you about Ben?" Tears of anger sprang to her eyes. Here she was face to face with the madman that tried to kill him. She felt a very strong need to scratch his eyeballs out of head.

"Oh, no, don't cry," he shushed her, like she was a child. "It's all over Hollywood, of course. He overdosed on drugs… morphine I believe the rumor was."

He placed an arm around her shoulders. "Come, darling, I'll tell you all about it." Turning her, he tried to direct her to the side of the yard near the bushes.

***

Ben saw everything happen. He'd never make it in time to get to her side. He called on the next best thing. "Brutus, go to Abbi!"

That was all the dog needed to hear, as he darted to his mistress.

***

Abbi shrugged his arm off in revulsion. "No!" She gagged at his touch.

Recovering quickly, she smiled. "No, it's fine, we can talk here."

"But it's more private over there." He pointed to the stand of trees. "In case you need a friendly shoulder to cry on."

"Nope! I'm good," she said, shaking her head.

"Abbi, nothing will happen. You're safe with me," he smiled charmingly.

She felt like she was going to vomit. If she did, she'd be sure to aim it at his hateful face.

He started tugging on her arm, attempting to drag her away.

"I said, no!" She wrenched her arm free, taking off towards Kim and Steve's direction. She hadn't even taken a step before she felt his arm snake around her waist, lifting her off the ground as the other came around to cover her mouth. She heard a low warning growl, of an approaching attack. *Brutus*! Hope welled up inside her as she heard a howl of pain before she was dropped to the ground. She quickly scrambled away, turning to see Brutus sink his teeth firmly into Raven's backside.

"Brutus! Stand down," Ben commanded as he came to Abbi's side, helping her off the ground.

Raven stumbled back as if he saw a ghost. "Y... you... you're dead, I poisoned you myself!" he stammered.

"Evidently I'm not. No thanks to you," Ben sneered, flexing his fists. He so wanted to beat the shit out of Raven but restrained himself from doing so.

Ava and Mark came running up along with Steve and Kim. Abbi glanced at the lake as the police boat came to shore.

"We have Raven's confession on tape, all of it," Steve said.

Raven lunged at Abbi. "You're too good for the likes of him." He pawed at her. When she jumped away from his advances, he resorted to calling her names.

"That's it." Ben had had it with this guy. He grabbed him by the shirt with his left hand, drew back with his right, and smashed his fist into Raven's face.

Dropping to the ground from the force of impact, Raven screamed in pain.

Once wasn't enough. Blinded by fury, Ben pounced on him, smashing his fist again and again against Raven's face. He thought of all the times Raven had terrified Abbi. He wanted to cause him as much pain as he put her through.

Abbi wanted to grab Ben, but she was afraid she wouldn't get through to him. "Ben! Please stop!" Abbi pleaded. "Mark! Stop him!" she yelled.

Abbi's voice was the only thing that he heard. Ben grabbed Raven's shirt, lifting his torso off the ground. Their faces mere inches away, Ben sneered, "Consider yourself lucky that she stopped me," he flung him away in disgust.

Mark grabbed Ben under the arms, dragging him away.

Ben shrugged him off, searching for Abbi in the gathering crowd.

Abbi rushed to Ben's side, cradling his bruised and bloody hands in her own. "Oh God. Why did you go and do that?" She looked at him with tears in her eyes. "Let's get you inside." She ushered him towards the house.

Steve noticed Raven getting up off the ground, saw that he was struggling to get something out of his pocket. Pulling a gun out, Raven aimed at Ben's retreating back. Steve tackled him to the ground before he could get a shot off. The gun flew, landing at Kim's feet.

Abbi and Ben, none the wiser continued to the house. When they heard someone calling to him… a female, Abbi noted. On the steps, she glanced back to see Lorna trying to catch up with them, followed by Mark and Ava.

Ben stopped. Looking back, he said, "Not now, Lorna." He didn't have any fight left in him.

"Please. I just had to come here for myself, to see. Raven told me you had died," she said with a cry.

He put an arm around Abbi's waist. "As you can see, I'm alive, and well," he sighed.

Lorna arched a brow, giving a pointed look at where Ben had placed his arm. "I see," she said; spinning on her heel, she stormed away.

"Come on, let's get you cleaned up," Abbi mumbled, taking his hand, leading him into the house.

"Sit." She pointed to the table on her way to the bathroom to get the first aid kit.

Ben pulled the chair out with his foot. Sitting down hard, he looked at his hands. He wasn't sure if it was his blood or Raven's… both he supposed.

If Raven had just kept his mouth shut.

They throbbed, but he'd do it all over again to protect Abbi. She came into the kitchen at that moment. Ben watched as she sat the kit on the table and hurried over to the fridge. He chuckled when he saw the bag of frozen peas, she wrapped in a towel again. She had nursed his wounds more than his mother ever had needed to. He sent her a lazy smile when she took the chair opposite of him. She took his right hand in hers. Her head bent, she looked up at him. "This will sting."

"Go ahead, love."

She gently wiped the dried blood away with a damp cloth. He watched her as she took a medical pad from the kit. Ripping it open, she soaked it in disinfectant. Her hand poised over his skin, glancing up. She looked to see if he was ready. At his quick nod, she gently pressed it to his wounds.

Ben just about shot through the roof. The sting was so intense; he felt like vomiting. Sucking in a breath, he dared not move.

"I'm so sorry," Abbi softly said. She tried to be as gentle as she could, but try as she might, she knew she was causing him more pain. She quickly removed the cap on the antibiotic tube. Squirting in on his hand, she smoothed it with her finger. Taking a roll of gauze, she carefully wrapped it around each finger, across his knuckles, and wound it around his hand, taping it in place. She studied her handiwork. "There how does that feel?"

"Better. Thanks, love." He said, flexing his hand. "The other is fine, just bloody, is all."

Getting up, she took him by the hand. "Come along," she said, walking to the sink. Turning the tap, she shoved his hand under the running water, lathering it up with dish soap.

A knock on her back door, had her yelling, "Come in."

Ben looked around to see Steve with a uniformed officer standing there. "Hey Steve," he said as he nodded, to the cop.

Abbi turned just then, smiling a greeting to both.

"Hey, Ben," he nodded. Looking to the man beside him he said, "This is officer Vince Scott. We just wanted to let you and Abbi know that Raven Black is being charged with attempted murder, assault, assault with a weapon, and uttering threats. The list goes on, but that's the gist of it."

Kim came around the corner just then laughing. "Man, that

was great!" At their confused looks, she said, "Oh yeah! After you guys came in here. Your dogs went after Raven," she laughed again.

"What?" Abbi cried in alarm, darting a concerned look at the dogs that were now lying on the floor chewing on a bone.

"Yeah, Molly went up to him, sniffed him, then she squatted... pissed right on his face," Kim cackled. "He tried getting up and kicking her... until Brutus bit his balls." She was now smacking her leg as the tears streamed down her face.

Ben laughed as the image flitted through his mind, Raven deserved everything he got.

Another officer came around the corner. "Vince, we are ready to roll." Nodding to everyone, he turned and left.

Ben stepped forward, half expecting Vince to arrest him for assault. "Is everything okay?" he asked, ready to face the consequences.

"Yeah, no worries, we all agree your actions were justified." Vince told him, extending his hand to Ben.

Relieved, Ben thanked him as he shook the officer's hand.

"No problem," he said. Nodding his head to Abbi, "Ma'am," he touched his hat, turning to leave.

"I'll walk you out," Steve said, following him.

"So now what, guys?" Kim asked.

Abbi looked at her as Ben snaked his arm around her waist. He bent to nuzzle the soft spot just below her ear. His breath hot against her neck sent shivers up her spine. "How does a bath sound... hmm?" he murmured. She leaned back, smiling she gave him a slow nod. They turned, walking down the hall to Abbi's room.

"Hey! Where are you guys going? The party is still going on..."

Kim watched as they walked, their lips locked together the whole time. "…. Guys?"

The only answer she received was the soft thud of the bedroom door.

Chapter 16

Abbi sat in front of her computer, just finishing up her last chapter.

Finally! She thought as she typed the last word. She sat back staring at the screen, thinking how only six months ago she had been struggling with every word she typed. *Odd how life turns out,* she thought.

Brutus' loud yawn had her glancing at him as he laid in the sun, Molly and Lucy were at his side. She got up, walking to the control panel for the wall of windows. She opened one, allowing the crisp air outside to come in. She marveled at the view of the lake they provided. It was a picture-perfect day, blue skies, brilliant sunshine, the fall colours were spectacular this year. She couldn't wait until it snowed. She could see it already in her mind. The lake frozen, the sun sparkling off the snow-covered pine trees.

Ben had been right. This was the perfect room for her to write in. They had used his bedroom until they had completed the addition. Ben got the bathroom he wanted. He claimed it was for Abbi, but she secretly knew different. And she got the bedroom of her dreams. Not that she hadn't already had that, but this one was for them both this time. She smiled, at how excited he was to design it all himself, with her input of course.

She moved into his home the week after her party. She frowned, thinking back to the BBQ... not realizing at the time, how close Ben had come to being shot. Thank God, Steve saw Raven's intentions. Otherwise, she very well could have lost him that day. The thought drove her nearly to the edge of insanity.

If Raven had succeeded, she'd be the one sitting in a jail cell now. As it was, Raven's case was before the courts. The Crown Attorney was pushing for life. She just hoped to God he got it, for all he had done… especially to Ben.

Oh, how she missed him! He'd been away for a month and a half now. Him and Mark had been off shooting another movie. This time a comedy, both having main roles in it. That was another thing… Mark had convinced Abbi to let him rent her house. He told her he had two willing roommates to move in with him as well. So, it would never stand empty as this one had.

Ava and Kim both shocked the hell out of her when they announced they were staying in Pearl Lake. Ava had sold her spa in Windsor and opened a new one on the edge of the village in a gorgeous Victorian home. And Kim, she was assisting Doc Spence at the clinic. Her reason for staying was she couldn't bring herself to leave her partners in crime. Abbi chuckled at the thought of what those three had gotten up to in the past few months.

Sighing, she looked at her watch. *Just a few more hours…* Ben would stroll through the door and take her in his arms. A thrill went through her body at the thought of it. Their flight took off 8 hours ago from somewhere in South America. She had such an uneasy feeling whenever he was flying. He always reassured her that nothing would go wrong, but it didn't help any.

Hmm, I should know what country they are coming from. She'd just turned to look at the itinerary of their trip sitting on her desk, when she heard a car flying into the driveway. *Ben, he must be home earlier than he thought!* She rushed to the window, frowning as she saw Ava's car come to a sliding halt.

That's odd. Turning from the window, she crossed the room at a hurried pace. Crossing the walkway to the stairs, her foot touching the bottom step just as the front door flew open.

Ava stood there panting for a moment, her face pale.

"Ava? Honey, are you sick? What's wrong?" Abbi felt sick herself at that very moment.

Shaking her head, panting she said, "I tried to get here as fast as I could. Why didn't you answer your phone?"

"I was writing. I have it on silent? What's going on?"

Ava waved her hand. "It's all over the news. Turn on the TV," she said. Hurrying into the living room Abbi grabbed the remote, stabbing the power button on.

There before them on the screen was a live viewing of plane wreckage. With a sinking feeling, Abbi sat down on the arm of the couch. "Ava... what are you trying to tell me..." She knew exactly what she was trying to tell her. Her brain, however, needed to hear it, as her heart was in denial.

Ava turned to her mother, her tears streaming down her face.

"Mom," she went to her then. "Ben and Mark's plane went down twenty minutes after takeoff."

***

"…. Ben?" Mark swallowed hard. His throat felt like he hadn't had a drink of anything in a week. "Buddy… can you hear me?" He lay still on the ground. Straining to hear anything. Only silence met his ears. Slowly moving, he tested each limb to see if anything was broken. His left wrist was the only thing that hurt like a bitch.

A loud screech broke through the silence causing him to jerk straight up. He sat, gazing around at his surroundings for any signs of life. *Where the hell is Ben? And why am I sitting on the ground in the middle of a forest?* He remembered now. They were on their way back to Canada when the plane started to shake and shudder.

He had glanced to his left, seeing Ben with his cellphone in his hand. He had looked at him, both knowing the peril they were in, knowing this could be the end. "I had to send Abbi a text to tell her one last time that I love her."

Mark had scoffed at him, trying to reassure him that they would get through this… despite him having doubts to the contrary. "Man, everything will be fine. We will be back home in no time. And you can ask to marry her like you planned." Mark put an arm around Ben then, both men hugging.

They felt the plane rapidly falling to earth. The air masks dropped, both grabbed for them, putting them on. Being frequent flyers, they knew the drill, as they ducked and tucked their heads between their legs. A sound of metal ripping and roaring wind was the only sign that it had damaged the plane as it grazed the treetops. Their section landed with a sickening crash of metal on branches.

The next thing Mark remembered was calling out to Ben. Panic started to set in with the realization that he might be the only survivor… until he heard a faint groan.

Mark stood up looking around. Luggage, metal, trees, and… bodies were strewn about him. He caught movement out of the corner of his eye. Rushing over he saw a woman still strapped in her seat. "Miss, are you okay?" Mark asked, concerned when he saw the gash on her brow, blood pooling into her eye. Looking around for something clean, he tore open the nearest suitcase. Grabbing a t-shirt he ripped it into a makeshift bandage wrapping it around her head. He unbuckled her from her seat and laid her on the ground, telling her to lay still.

He went to the next victim. Finding the man to be fine except for a few bumps and bruises, he learned his name was Hank. Together they started helping others.

After a while, Mark still hadn't come across Ben. He saw there was one more person needing help… and they weren't moving. He made his way over to them, seeing that they were wearing the same colour of jeans Ben had on. Mark had to stop for a minute, steeling himself for what he may find. He slowly went to the person. It relieved him to see that it wasn't Ben, but instantly he was filled with sadness. The person hadn't made it.

Mark hurried back to the others. "Hey, Hank. Did you come across a man, brown hair, about yay high? Speaks with a British accent?"

"No, sorry, I didn't…" Hank replied, earnestly.

"Thanks, man." Mark turned away, glancing around, in case he missed someone laying there. He stood with his hands on his hips. Worriedly, he muttered aloud, "Ben… Where the hell are you, buddy?"

***

Abbi didn't hear Ava. She focused her eyes and ears on the reporter's sober tone: "The cast and crew of Stoned River's plane crashed shortly after takeoff."

Photos of the plane were now on the screen as the reporter continued. "It's confirmed that cast members Ben Quinn and Mark Donovan were to be on this flight that was en route to Toronto."

Their photos were now on the screen. Abbi got up walking to the TV. She laid her hand on Ben's photo, the tears now falling from her eyes.

"There have been some casualties, but at this time we aren't sure if they are among those who perished in this tragic accident."

Abbi put her hand down. She stood there looking at the TV.

Wouldn't I know if he was gone? She didn't believe it. She refused to believe it after everything they had gone through… she *would* know.

"Mom?" Ava sniffled, putting a hand on Abbi's arm. "Are you okay?"

Abbi turned, looking at her. "Yes honey, I'm fine." Taking a steadying breath, Abbi knew what she had to do. "Ava, go pack a bag."

Ava gaped at her. *Oh my God, she's lost it.* Shaking her head in confusion, she said, "What?"

"I said… go pack a bag. We are going to that plane wreck. I'll call Kim. Both of you better be ready in a half-hour, or I'm leaving without you," she said, pulling out her phone.

She hated flying. Ben knew that. When he had to go back to Madrid, to finish up his scenes for The Jasper Killings, true to her promise, she begrudgingly went with him… Tears formed in her eyes as her mind replayed the beautiful memories, they made there. She, of course, was drunk as a skunk on the flights there and back. Thank God he was there to take care of her. Otherwise, she'd never have returned to Canada.

She chewed her bottom lip, waiting for Kim to pick up. "Hey, Kim…"

"Hey, Abbi, did you hear…"

Abbi cut her off. They didn't have time for that. "Yes, I heard. Ava came by and told me. Can you ask Doc to stop by and check on the dogs for me? Better yet, ask him to stay here for a while? I have no idea how long we will be." She paused listening to the exchange in the background.

"Uh, Abbi… he wants to know… who is we?"

"Tell him we as in you, Ava and me. We are going down there to find them."

"She told me to tell you that 'we' is me, Ava and her and… wait… *what*?" Kim yelled into the phone.

"Be ready in ten minutes. Ava is packing for you, as we

speak." She hung up with Kim still jabbering.

She looked through her contact list. Stabbing the digits, she waited for it to connect.

"Nigel. Abbi Peterson here. I need you to find me a plane..." She listened... "No, not a rental. One for sale.... How soon? Oh, in about an hour I'll be in Toronto, can you make it happen? Great, and make sure a pilot goes with it... a very experienced one, please. Right! I'll get Ava to transfer the money on the way down. Thanks, Nigel" She hung up the phone.

Sending a prayer to the powers that be, she swallowed hard at what she was about to undertake. Speaking aloud she said, "Ben..." She had to pause. The lump in her throat caused her voice to crack as the tears streamed down her face. She had to continue, maybe just maybe he would hear her voice. Heaving a big sigh, she cleared her throat. "I'm on my way. Please, babe be safe. I know you're out there, somewhere..."

She grabbed her keys, kissed each animal on the head, telling them to be good, and headed out the door. She knew she was crazy for doing this, but she'd be crazy not to. She refused to give up on the one man who had changed her life so completely... one who loved her with his very soul. Ben had once promised her he'd follow her to the ends of the earth. She just never told him that she'd do the same.

Moonlit Stalker

Dear Readers,

As a child, I would write plays that I would subject my family to. I would act them out behind my father's lazy boy using my stuffed animals as the characters. My family would sit and watch while I "performed". They had no clue what was going on, and likely I didn't either. But nonetheless they sat patiently watching. Or at least I think they did (I had no clue; I was behind the chair).

    Since I picked up my first historical romance, I knew I wanted to write a book one day. The only thing that stopped me was someone saying I couldn't. That was it. I figured they were right... I couldn't write. That was 28 years ago now, and every day I regretted at least not trying. I would attempt it, but their words always reared their ugly head again, and I would give up. Finally, I decided I had nothing to lose but my regret. And so, Abbi and Ben's story came to life. I didn't need an outline, or a plot or even a list of characters. They have been with me for 28 years. As silly as it sounds, they told me their story, and it HAD to be written. And so, I invite you to come along on this journey with me. My only hope is that you enjoy reading it as much as I have writing it.

    If you have gotten this far, I thank you and hope you have enjoyed the beginning of Abbi and Ben's adventures. I invite you to a preview of their story continuation, Moonlit Road: Book 3 of Pearl Lake, The Moonlit Trilogy. ~ Tina Marie

For inquires please email at:

pearllakethemoonlittrilogy@gmail.com

ACKNOWLEDGEMENTS

First, to my husband Pat, I'm sorry for drowning out your talking with music playing in my ears, but I can't listen to you and write at the same time, haha. Thank you for knowing how important these books are to me. To my kids, Jonathan and Amanda, even though you're both adults and have families of your own, you two are still my world and I thank you both for being who you are.

To my sisters, Laura and Deb. Laura thank you for not only editing my book but also for putting up with my endless rewrites… constantly. Deb, you read faster than I can write! Thanks for always believing in me and knowing from the time I was a teenager that I had these book in me, I just needed the time to convince myself! To my brother in law Pat. You were so in awe of the leaves that I had made, I can only imagine your reaction to these books, haha, P.S. We all miss you down here. To my parents. Mom, thank you for putting up with the endless questions .and actually watching when I acted out plays that I had written, when I was too young to even know what words were. To my Dad, I have learned so much from you. From learning how to shingle and tar a roof to driving a car at 14. Some of my fondest memories are of me tagging along behind you. I have always admired how your mind works and I like to think mine is the same. You both have always been there for me no matter what, and I shall do the same for you. To my brother Ralph and sister in law Donna and the kids. It's been so long that I have seen all of you. But not a day goes by that I haven't thought of you in some small way in the last 29 years. I miss yous more than words could ever describe.

Chapter 1

"Abbi! For God's sake, slow the hell down!" Kim yelled from the back seat for the tenth time.

Abbi was zoned out. And just like the last time Kim went on a tirade, she was ignored. If anything, it made Abbi want to go faster. Zipping past the cars and transports, her only thought was she needed to get to Ben and now.

The plan had been to fly. Nigel, her real estate agent had 'connections' and had assured her that he could find her a jet; and he did, but not for at least a week. God Himself couldn't keep her waiting for a week. They had to leave now. Their only option was to drive. Abbi hated travelling on the 401 almost as much as she hated flying. But nothing was going to stop her. Not even her fear. She gripped the steering wheel a little tighter as she read the sign on the side of the road. London, population 353 000, 4 interchanges.

Great. Just what I need. Traffic is going to pick up again…

"Mom?" Ava's, soft voice broke into her musings.

"Yeah?" Abbi responded, never taking her eyes off the road.

Ava knew that look on her mother's face and it wasn't good. They'd been on the road now for 5 hours. Traffic had been brutal through Toronto. But that hadn't stopped her mother from keeping the speed at a constant 130 km. She had to be getting tired.

"Why don't we stop for a minute? There's a service station just past London. We can grab a bite to eat and a coffee." Ava suggested.

"Yeah, and I really need to take a piss." Kim chimed in from the back seat, groaning her need.

Abbi adjusted the rear-view mirror until she caught Kim's image in the reflection. She *was* squirming an awful lot.

"Fine. Five minutes and we're back on the road," Abbi agreed. She hated the thought of even stopping for five minutes. That was five minutes too long. But she had to admit she needed to make a pit stop to the ladies' room herself.

It was starting to get dark. The city lights of London were now behind them as Abbi stepped on the gas pedal. The sooner they got there, the sooner they could leave.

Ava and Kim grabbed the 'oh shit' bars as the SUV swerved around a transport. Flying past it, they all failed to see the OPP cruiser right in front of it.

"Son of a bitch!" Abbi swore as the cruiser's lights engaged.

The signs for the service station were right there. Just 5 more kms to go. She had to stop. And she would… at the service station. Never batting an eye, Abbi kept her speed steady, mentally counting down each km.

Abbi flipped her lid; Kim just knew it. "Uh… Abbi? You gonna stop or what?" she asked.

"Mom?! Pull over before you get yourself arrested." Ava implored.

There! Thank. God. There's the merge lane for the service station.

Abbi quickly clicked on her signal. Slowing down, she exited the highway and rolled to a stop in an open area of the parking lot.

"Jesus, Abbi what the hell were you thinking?" Kim asked, shaking her head.

With a heavy sigh, Abbi rummaged in the center console for her ownership and insurance.

"I'm not... thinking that is." She shot a quick glance to her two companions. "If I don't get arrested. One of you will need to drive. I um... I need a break." She whispered, her voice cracking at her admission.

"Sure, honey." Kim's voice softened. "One of us will drive, won't we Ava?"

"Yeah mom, we can take turns." Ava reached over giving her mom a hug.

A sharp knock on Abbi's window had them all jumping. Turning to look out the glass Abbi saw the police officer standing there. She hit the window's power button. As it lowered, she glanced up at the angry face peering down at her.

"Ma'am... license and registration, please."

Without a word, Abbi handed over the requested documents.

"You do realize you were going 140, right? I could haul you in for stunt driving and impound your car. Mind telling me what's so important that you're willing to risk the lives of others on the road and your passengers?" the officer asked, bending down to look at Ava and Kim.

"Ah..." Abbi started to speak and shut her mouth. She had no way of getting out of this, she was guilty as hell.

"Well, hello Officer." Kim could see clearly from the back seat how attractive the cop was. "You see, she's not in her right state of mind at the moment," Kim supplied, pointing to her head. She spun her finger in circles, silently conveying that Abbi was off her rocker. For good measure, she softly muttered "cuckoo" as she turned to look out her window.

The cop said in disbelief. "Is that so?"

Ava leaned across Abbi just then.

"What she means is, my mother... err... Abbi here," she jerked her head towards Abbi.

"Has had quite a shock. You see, there was a plane crash..."

The officer looked taken aback, frowning he looked between Ava and Kim. Ava immediately clamped her mouth shut.

She didn't want to say anything more, in case the officer decided to haul them all off to jail.

"Then why is she driving and one of you aren't?"

"She didn't ask?" Kim supplied, thinking he was insane for even suggesting it. One didn't tell Abbi what to do when she was in this state of mind. She'd bite their heads off if they did.

Abbi felt like a child at the moment. She had to say something, to fess up to her crime, speeding like a lunatic down the busiest highway in North America.

"Whoa, wait, hold up." Abbi held her hand up for some calm. She didn't feel very calm now, but she had to take control. "Officer. Wait, what is your name again?" she asked.

"I didn't say, Miss..." He pulled out a penlight, flashing the beam across her license.

Abbi was suddenly blinded by that same beam. She squinted from the onslaught of brightness.

"Abbi? Abbi Petersen, aka Abbi Stevens?"

She held up her hand, trying to shield her eyes. "Ahh... yes? Do I know you or something? Could you please get that light out of my face?" She blinked rapidly.

"Oh, shit... sorry. It's Noah. Noah Steel? We went to high school together." He grinned when the recognition hit Abbi's face.

With a squeal, Abbi grabbed her door handle, shoving it open, she unsuccessfully launched herself at Noah. Her actions halted by her seat belt.

"Some things never change, do they Abbs?" Noah bellowed. "Here, let me give you a hand." He leaned in, reaching over he unsnapped her belt.

Taking her hand, he guided her out of the vehicle and into his arms.

"What?!" Ava and Kim cried in unison, gaping at the couple as they embraced.

"Uh… Aunt Kim… are you seeing what I'm seeing?" Ava whispered in disbelief.

Kim just stared with her mouth agape.

Ava snapped her eyes to Kim. "Did you know about this and not tell me?!" She hissed, before turning back to couple embracing.

"How the hell would I know? They… they seem to *know* each other. If you catch my drift." Kim stammered.

"Yeah. What do you think we should do?" Fearing she would miss something. Ava risked another glance at Kim.

"I don't know…" Yanking on her door handle Kim said, "Let's go, we need to intervene."

"Wait for me!" Ava scrambled out her door, rounded the front of the SUV and abruptly plowed into Kim's back.

"Jesus, Mary and Joseph," Kim muttered under her breath. There before them stood Abbi and the officer… Noah. Talking in hushed tones. Abbi crying, and Noah comforting her.

"No, no, no!! This is not a good thing." Ava stated as she watched shaking her head. She gave Kim a shove, "*Stop* them!"

"Me?! Why me?! She's *your* mother."

"You've known her longer, besides, she's used to you butting in." Ava stated.

"Fine… but you're coming with me."

Together, they moved as one until they stood within earshot. Shifting from one foot to the other Kim took a deep breath and said, "Ahem. Abbi? Honey. We need to finish up here if you want to get to Ben. You *do* remember *Ben*… don't you?" Kim scooted closer, talking in a soothing tone.

Abbi swallowed hard; her eyes red from crying. She backed away from Noah, wiping her tears off his jacket she nodded, not trusting herself to speak just yet.

Kim had never seen Abbi so upset before in her life. Wait. No that wasn't true. When Ben had almost died, from being drugged was the worst she'd seen her sister. She didn't know if Abbi was upset now because of Ben or from seeing Noah suddenly in her life again. Seeing how this was the first time Kim had the privilege of laying her eyes on the officer, she wasn't entirely sure what Noah meant to Abbi. One thing she was certain of was that it ended here and now.

Noah caught the emphasis on Ben's name. "Kim, is it?" At her nod he continued. "Abbi was just telling me about Ben. I can understand why you guys are in a rush, that's why I offered to escort your vehicle to Windsor. I can only go as far as the Ambassador Bridge. But on one condition." Noah looked at Ava and Kim.

Both had the 'caught in the headlights' look of a deer on the side of a darkened road.

"Noah doesn't want me driving." Abbi explained, finally breaking her silence.

"Of course not!!" both women exclaimed, relief evident on their faces as they rushed over to hug Abbi.

"Then it's settled. I'll just radio into dispatch; explain the situation, while you all go do your business in there." Noah pointed to the service station.

"I was afraid I'd have to get physical with you Noah... err... Officer... Noah. I'll just shut up now," Kim giggled. *I really needed to learn to keep my mouth shut*, she thought, as she felt the blush rise to her cheeks. "Well, you know... Abbi and Ben..." she tried to smooth her outburst over.

"I do, and Abbi and I have always been just friends. Right Abbs?"

Abbi smiled and nodded. She still didn't trust herself to speak too much. She felt she was on the edge of a meltdown and that wouldn't do. She had to find Ben. Even if it meant… *NO!! You're not going there, Abbi!! He's alive…*

"Come on, Mom, let's get something to eat." Ava put an arm around her, guiding her toward the building while Kim followed staring at the police officer with a dreamy look in her eyes.

Abbi sat with her head in her hands at the table waiting for Ava and Kim to return with food. She laid her purse on the table and planted her face on it. She didn't care that people were shooting strange looks her way. She was so unbelievably spent. If she had the strength, she might have just shot them back a look or two… or given them the one-finger salute.

Abbi, that's not like you at all, she thought, as her purse vibrated against her face. *What the hell is that?* She sat straight up. Rummaging through it to find the culprit, her hand grabbed the object.

My phone? She never had the sound on, let alone vibrate… *Ava, she must have turned it on.* Tapping the screen, she saw there were a couple of texts and 10 missed calls. She scrolled through the call log.

Oh, my God. It's Mark! With shaking hands, Abbi quickly stabbed his number. He picked up after the second ring.

Not stopping to exchange pleasantries she cut to the chase, "Mark, it's Abbi, is Ben with you?" She closed her eyes waiting.

"Hey, Abbi. Uh, how's it going?" He sounded so… distraught.

"Mark… where are you? Is Ben with you?"

"I guess you heard about the plane crash, huh?"

Why is he beating around the bush…? She took a calming breath. "Yes, I did. It's all over the news. But where are you now?"

"Me? I'm at the hospital. They are keeping me for observation… just for the night," he told her.

"Where is Ben? Is he with you?" She knew he wasn't, but she had to hear it before she would admit it to herself.

"Ben? Umm…"

"Spit it out for cripes sake or I'll rip you a new asshole when I see you next!" she shouted into the phone.

Her tirade caused everyone to look her way, including Ava, Kim and Noah.

"Oh, oh…" Kim said with dread.

"I'm on it," Ava replied, as she spun on her heel, running towards her mom.

Abbi was apologizing to Mark for her outburst when Ava arrived at the table. She motioned for her to give her the phone.

"Mark, I'm so sorry. I need answers and no one seems to know them… Ava wants to talk to you." Abbi handed over her phone as she got up from the table. She headed to the washroom, the only place she could escape to. Pushing open the first stall door, she locked it and sat heavily on the toilet, bursting into tears.

Kim came to the table with a tray of drinks in her hands. Noah following close behind with bags of food.

"Where's your mom?" she asked, glancing around as she sat the tray on the table.

"She went to the washroom. I just got off the phone with Mark." Ava said.

"And?" Kim hedged, as she stuck straws in the drinks.

"He's in the hospital, just overnight… for observation. He should be released tomorrow if all goes well…"

"Ok, so where did the plane go down?" Noah asked.

"Mark was told about 60 miles south of Gatlinburg, Tennessee, near a little mountain town called Cooper's Hill."

"And... Ben?" Kim held her breath waiting for the response. She didn't know what they would do with Abbi if it wasn't good.

"Ben is nowhere to be found." Ava looked at Kim and Noah.

"What do you mean nowhere to be found?!" Abbi asked in disbelief. No one had seen her return. "Give me my phone Ava." Abbi thrust out a shaky hand.

"Mom, Mark said he looked everywhere. And so, did the police. It's like he just vanished into thin air."

By that time, Abbi wasn't listening. She tapped her screen, going instantly to the text messages... Ben. He had sent her two. The first she read with tears swimming in her eyes.

'Abbi. Love. It's me. Things aren't looking so good for Mark and me. I won't go into details. I know I've told you this before, but please, always remember that you captured my heart from the second we met. You are the best thing that has ever happened to me. I have no regrets with you, love. No matter what happens, know that I'll always love you. Forever yours, Ben.'

Abbi had to sit down before she fainted. Taking a steadying breath, she continued to read the second one...

'Hello there, Abbi I presume. I'm not sure who this is. But from the last message I sent you, I'm confident that we know each other... intimately. I seem to be in some need of assistance but have no idea where I am. Can you please advise. Thanks, Benjamin Quinn'.

Abbi started giggling. Softly at first, then full out laughing hysterically. It really wasn't funny, of course. Ben had no clue who she was, but she couldn't help herself. She knew it! He was alive!

"What's so funny?" Noah asked.

Between the tears slipping down her cheeks and her hysterical laughing, everyone at the table thought she had finally lost it.

"Ahh…" She wiped the tears away with her sleeve. "He's alive…" was all she could manage to say.

"Mark is, yes… we know that mom."

Abbi shook her head; she shoved her phone to the center of the table. "Not Mark, Ava. Ben… he's alive," Abbi said as she broke down in sobs of relief.

True to his word, Noah was in the lead, sirens blaring and lights flashing. They were en route to Windsor, with Ava at the wheel, just passing through Chatham Kent.

Abbi texted Ben back, after attempts to reach him by phone had failed. After 20 minutes he had responded, telling her that he was injured. A broken leg, he was sure and slipping in and out of consciousness. Abbi had immediately called 911, telling them she was talking to Ben via text. They said they could contact his phone provider and narrow down the pings on the towers around the vicinity of the plane crash, but he had to make a call first.

Her last text to him, she told him that it was imperative that he call her. Abbi leaned her head back, staring blankly at the night sky through the SUV's glass top roof. Despite her protests, they'd decided to stay the night in Windsor. Luke and Lane were both out of town on business and so they had little choice but to stay in a hotel. Still a 45 min drive away. They still had 9 hours of driving ahead of them in the States. She hated to waste time on sleeping.

She would see, she may just leave in the middle of the night… without Ava and Kim.

Chapter 2

Ben woke with a start to find that a light dusting of snow covered him. *Where the hell am I? Now that's a question that may never get answered*, he thought wryly, as he laid a hand on his leg. He knew it was banged up bad, likely broken. He also knew that if he didn't get out of there and soon, he wouldn't make it. If only he could find something that resembled a crutch, maybe just maybe he could get the hell out of there. It would have to wait till daylight though. The moon barely gave off enough light to see through the leafless trees.

A twig snapping had him whipping his head around to the sound. Something was out there. He heard it, and he felt like he was being watched. Whatever it was, it didn't come close enough to get a good look at it. Likely a raccoon. He hoped. Then again, he could have just imagined it. His mind had been playing tricks on him, since the second he had woken up laying on the forest floor. The first time, he'd heard a woman's voice in his mind, made him think he was going crazy. Now, he looked forward to it.

He touched his fingers to the bump on his forehead, wincing from the pain. He tried to remember what had happened. He knew from the sickening screech of metal that played on repeat in his mind that he was in a plane crash. From the looks of it, he had been the only occupant, or so he thought. It was the only thing he was certain of… that and his name.

Shivering against the cold, he closed his eyes, trying desperately to remember what his life was like. He had looked at the photos on his phone endlessly. There were pictures of a lake, and a house in the middle of renovations, pictures of him and a beautiful woman together, some of just her alone. He knew they were a couple; he could feel it in his gut, but he simply couldn't remember her.

Abbi was her name. The photo attached to her name and phone number told him so. He also knew deep down; she meant the world to him. Ben wished he could remember her. The feel of her skin, her laugh, her voice, anything that would bring a hint of what he had meant to her. Did she love him? God, he hoped so. He could feel himself drifting off again. The image of Abbi burning into his mind was his last thought before the darkness overtook him.

The buzzing of his phone had him jerking awake. It was Abbi. He squinted trying desperately to focus on the words in the text. *'Ben, please call me. I need you to call. The police can trace your cell off the towers. But you have to call.'*

He hit the phone icon as his teeth started to chatter. He waited shivering uncontrollably, praying the call would go through this time.

"Ben?"

He heard a soft voice in his ear. The same voice he had heard in his mind repeatedly.

"Abbi, is that you?" His voice broke on her name; memories of her, of them, flashed through his mind.

He could hear her crying softly.

"Love, please don't cry. I'm fine. Just a bit banged up is all."

"You called me love, does that mean...?" she trailed off.

"Yeah, I remember. I could never forget you for long Abbi."

She let out a shaky breath, half laughing half crying.

He remembered how beautiful she was with tears streaming down her face. He wanted nothing more than to kiss them away.

"Mark is in the hospital in Gatlinburg. Ava and Kim have no idea, but I'm on my way to you. They'll know once they wake up.

I'm headed to the Detroit airport right now. Hang on a second."

He heard a sharp whistle, and her hailing for a taxi. A muffling sound came through the speaker as she told her destination to the driver. "I'm back. I should be there in an hour and a half." She panted out of breath.

Ben had no idea who Mark was, and who was Ava and Kim? Hell, he didn't even know who his own family was, for that matter. All he knew was Abbi and she was coming for him.

"Wait, you're going to fly... alone?" he asked her.

Softly Abbi said, "Nothing is stopping me from getting to you."

The determination in her voice made his heart swell. Knowing what she was about to embark on, he loved her more in that moment than he had ever loved another.

Swallowing hard, he said, "Love, I'm about to pass out I think...."

He lied, wanting to spare her from his emotions. He hated to end the call, but he had to.

"Ben... No!! Stay with me! Don't you dare fall asleep on me now!!"

He had to chuckle at the fire in her voice.

"Fine, love, just keep talking to me. Tell me what you've been up to. I'll try to stay awake. It's just so bloody cold out here." He mumbled, just as he heard the crack of branches breaking.

"What the hell was that?!" Abbi screeched. He was hoping she hadn't heard it; he could feel the panic in her voice through the phone.

Lights blinded Ben. He had no idea what it was other than it was a club cab pickup truck with a loud muffler. He quickly switched his phone to record, stuffing it and Abbi in his pocket.

"See Dean, I told you it was that Hollywood actor, sitting here in the middle of these trees."

How the hell did they find me? All Ben could see in any direction was endless forest. Really at that point he didn't care, he would be back to civilization soon, back to Abbi. He could make out two figures, both skinny as bean poles. Relief spread through him; he was saved. It came as a bit of a shock that they thought he was an actor though. The thought was absurd in his rattled mind.

"For once in your pathetic life Smitty, you're right. Come on. Let's get him loaded into the back of the truck." The one called Dean stalked over to Ben.

"Uh, how do you know me?" Ben asked the one named Smitty.

Smitty snorted. "Man, there isn't a person in the world who doesn't know who you are."

"I see." Ben said on a grimace as he was hoisted up by the armpits by both men.

"Can you walk?" Smitty asked trying to steady Ben.

"How dumb can you be? The man has been sitting here for hours. If he could walk, he would have left by now." Dean spat out at his companion as he gathered debris from the plane wreckage.

Smitty shrugged his shoulders as he put an arm around Ben's waist.

"Don't pay him no mind." Smitty muttered under his breath. "He's just pissed you landed in the middle of our farm."

Ben glanced around as he hobbled to the pickup truck and frowned, *Farm?* All he could see was barren trees for miles. *What the hell kind of farm is he referring to*, he wondered.

"Smitty, keep your trap shut." Dean growled as he brought up the rear. He walked to the bed of the truck and tossed his findings inside. Yanking open the driver's door, he grumbled, "We don't want Mr. Hollywood knowing anything… got it? Otherwise, he might just have to go missing again."

Smitty darted his eyes to Ben, "I'm sorry," he mumbled as he opened the backdoor for Ben. Both knowing what 'missing' meant.

Ben climbed into the backseat trying his damnedest to keep from bumping his leg. It was impossible for him not to grunt in pain when he settled on the seat.

"What's up with you?" Dean asked, turning to look at Ben.

With sweat beading on his brow, Ben pulled on his pant leg, tugging his leg into the truck he said, "Busted my leg in the crash,"

Dean sent him a sour look. "Great, just what we need."

"We can take you to the hospital, right?" Smitty looked to Dean for confirmation.

"Nope. Too much of a risk, someone is bound to recognize him." Dean hissed.

"We can't leave him to suffer…" Smitty reasoned.

"We'll get Murdock to look at him." Dean said starting the truck. "If she can't set it, well that's just too bad, isn't it?" He put the truck in gear and backed up.

Ben looked around. Trying to see anything that was a landmark as they sped through the forest. Trees and more trees met his eyes. Just his luck. His eyes grew large when he heard someone yelling from what sounded like far way.

What the hell? Shit, Abbi! He forgot she was still on the phone, no doubt hearing every word exchanged. Damn, she was going off on the other end. He quickly put his hand over his jeans pocket, fearing she would be heard. By feel, he disconnected the call, he hoped. He couldn't afford for the two in the front seat to know he had it. He needed his cell if he was ever going to be found.

The truck pulled up to what looked like an abandoned warehouse in the middle of the forest. *This does not look good.* There still wasn't a farm that Ben could see.

Dean killed the engine, looking over at Smitty, he jerked his head to the back seat where Ben sat.

"Get him inside, take him to Murdock. See if he can be fixed up."

"And if he can't? Then do we take him to the hospital?" Smitty asked.

"I don't know yet, I'll have to think about it. He should bring in a hefty price." Dean sneered.

Price? What the hell are they dealing here? Ben wondered.

"Right." Smitty nodded, as he opened his door and slammed it shut.

He came to Ben's door, opening it he said, "Come on, I'll get you looked at." Again, Ben couldn't help but groan in pain as Smitty helped him from the truck and to the building. The slightest movement of his leg made him want to vomit.

The smell caught Ben off guard. His first thought was that a family of skunks had taken up residence close by. As they drew closer to the building, the smell intensified.

Smitty guided Ben to a post. "Here, hang onto this while I open the door."

Ben gripped the post with one hand waiting for Smitty to open the door. He wished he could just take off. But he had a feeling that if he attempted it, a bullet would find its way into the back of his head. Nope. Better to play it safe, he had Abbi coming for him.

Funny, how a few months ago he wouldn't have even cared. *Holy shit!* he remembered what life was like before Abbi came into it. Merely existing. *Amazing how she'd changed it*, he thought, as Smitty shoved open the huge sliding door.

Ben's eyes grew large as light streamed from the open doorway. That wasn't a family of skunks he smelled a few minutes ago. That was the 'farm'. There stood before him, row after row, was the largest marijuana plants Ben had ever seen in his life. He let out a low whistle. He had no clue where he was but was pretty sure that what was before his eyes was an illegal grow op.

"Bloody hell…" Ben said in amazement.

"Pretty impressive, huh?" Smitty asked smiling, as he closed the door with a loud bang.

"Indeed, it is." Ben returned as he watched a worker walking around with a gun. One that he was sure was loaded. No. this wasn't good, not good at all.

The stakes just got higher. He had to come up with a plan and damn quick if he was ever going to get out of this alive….

Moonlit Road

What people are saying

One Moonlit Night, I loved this book. The characters kept me wanting to read more. I read constantly and this book captured me right from the beginning. I can't wait for the next one!

I haven't finished yet but has me not wanting to stop reading. It is captivating

Love love love it so far!! I'm not much of a reader but this book is catching my attention! Seriously can't put it down!! Book 2 hurry up

Yeah so, this story line is fantastic! Draws you right in. Zero clue who Tina Marie is but I'm always looking for book series. With twists. This has it! I usually don't bother with reviewing all my purchases, but I hope this lights a fire so book two comes out soon!

If book one is any indication. Then the story of these two is going to enthrall! A pretty quick read. Some twists and turns and a love story to boot! Love it

Manufactured by Amazon.ca
Bolton, ON